JOURNEY TO A STAR

The Marquis of Oakenshaw is asked by
the Foreign Secretary to visit Siam to
reassure the King who has been upset by
Britain and France quarrelling over the
frontiers.

A dashing, wealthy and handsome
bachelor, the Marquis asks several
friends to accompany him on his yacht,
including the latest Social Beauty – Lady
Bradwell.

At the last moment, Lady Bradwell,
having accepted excitedly, finds herself
owing to an accident, without a
lady's-maid. Her cousin Tarina also very
beautiful but extremely poor, agrees to
come with her under a disguised name.

How Tarina learns for the first time of
the intrigues and temptations of Society
but how she also lifts her eyes to the stars
is told in this 328th book by Barbara
Cartland.

Radio Operetta:

THE ROSE AND THE VIOLET (music by Mark Lubbock)
Performed in 1942.

Radio Plays:

THE CAGED BIRD: An episode in the Life of Elizabeth
Empress of Austria. Performed in 1957.

General:

BARBARA CARTLAND'S BOOK OF USELESS
INFORMATION, with a Foreword by The Earl
Mountbatten of Burma.
(In Aid of the United World Colleges.)

LOVE AND LOVERS (Picture Book)
THE LIGHT OF LOVE (Prayer Book)

BARBARA CARTLAND'S SCRAPBOOK,
(in Aid of the Royal Photographic Museum).
ROMANTIC ROYAL MARRIAGES
BARBARA CARTLAND'S BOOK OF CELEBRITIES

Verse:

LINES ON LIFE AND LOVE.

Music:

An Album of Love Songs sung with the Royal
Philharmonic Orchestra.

Film:

THE FLAME IS LOVE

Cartoons:

BARBARA CARTLAND ROMANCES (BOOK OF CARTOONS)
PUBLISHED IN GREAT BRITAIN, THE U.S.A., AND
OTHER PARTS OF THE WORLD.

Journey To A Star

Barbara Cartland

CORGI BOOKS

JOURNEY TO A STAR

A CORGI BOOK 0 552 12397 8

First publication in Great Britain

PRINTING HISTORY
Corgi edition published 1984

Copyright © Barbara Cartland 1984

This book is set in 10/11 Baskeville

Corgi Books are published by
Transworld Publishers Ltd.,
Century House, 61–63 Uxbridge Road,
Ealing, London W5 5SA

Made and printed in Great Britain by
Cox & Wyman Ltd., Reading, Berks.

About the Author

Barbara Cartland, the world's most famous romantic novelist, who is also an historian, playwright, lecturer, political speaker and television personality, has now written over 370 books and sold over 370 million over the world.

She has also had many historical works published and has written four autobiographies as well as the biographies of her mother and that of her brother, Ronald Cartland, who was the first Member of Parliament to be killed in the last war. This book has a preface of Sir Winston Churchill and has just been republished with an introduction by Sir Arthur Bryant.

She has recently completed a novel, 'Love at the Helm' with the help and inspiration of the late Admiral of the Fleet, the Earl Mountbatten of Burma. This is being sold for the Mountbatten Memorial Trust.

Miss Cartland in 1978 sang an Album of Love Songs with the Royal Philharmonic Orchestra.

In 1976 by writing twenty-one books, she broke the world record and has continued for the following seven years with 24, 20, 23, 24, 24, 25 and 22. In the Guinness Book of Records she is listed as the world's top-selling author.

In private life Barbara Cartland, who is a Dame of the Order of St. John of Jerusalem, Chairman of the St. John Council in Hertfordshire and Deputy President of the St. John Ambulance Brigade, has fought for better conditions and salaries for Midwives and Nurses.

She has championed the cause for old people, had the law altered regarding gypsies and founded the first Romany Gypsy camp in the world.

Barbara Cartland is deeply interested in Vitamin Therapy, and is President of the National Association for Health.

Her Designs "Decorating with Love" are being sold all over the U.S.A. and the National Home Fashions League made her, in 1981, "Woman of Achievement".

Fifty-four newspapers in the United States and several countries in Europe carry the strip cartoons of her novels.

Author's Note

The troubles in Siam over the frontiers which were acute in 1893 gradually subsided. In 1897 King Chulalongkorn and Queen Saowabha visited Europe travelling there and back in the yacht "*Maka Chakri*".

Their Majesties had a warm reception in France which surprised them. In England they stayed at Buckingham Palace and as the Queen was resting at Windsor in preparation for her Diamond Jubilee, they were received by the Prince of Wales (later Edward VII).

The great success of the tour which included Russia, Italy, Sweden and Belgium was that the King was the first Asian monarch who could talk to his hosts in English instead of through an interpreter.

When I was in Bangkok in 1982 I stayed at the new enlarged Oriental Hotel which is now one of the best hotels in the world. The river from my balcony was as exciting and entrancing as it has been for centuries and the Floating Market just as colourful as I have described it.

Unfortunately I did not have enough time to search for the Temple paintings of the Jataka tales. But there is a beautiful book of them called the "Ten Lives of The Buddha" by A.B. Criswold, which shows them in all their glorious colour.

CHAPTER ONE

1894

The Marquis of Oakenshaw yawned. It was very airless in St. James's Palace and the Levée was taking rather longer than usual.

The Prince of Wales was in a jovial mood and therefore talked to almost everyone who was presented to him and again and again his laughter rang out in the low-ceilinged chamber.

The Marquis who had seen it all happening before was not particularly impressed by the pageantry and the splendid appearance of the soldiers, sailors, Diplomats and Ministers present.

He was thinking that as it was an unusually sunny day for January he would much prefer to be in the country riding one of his spirited horses over the Park or racing some of his special friends on his private course.

He was so deep in his thoughts that he started when the Levée ended and the Prince of Wales began to move towards the door.

The Marquis hurried to his side, thinking as he did so that the Prince was growing more and more portly every year and there was no doubt that what he himself called his "Fancy clothes" would soon have to be replaced or let out.

The Marquis himself was very different.

As he liked to ride light and to race his own horses whenever possible, he kept his weight down.

This meant being abstemious when it came to the huge meals that were served at Marlborough House and by every hostess who wished to entertain the Prince of Wales's set.

The Marquis thought, again stifling a yawn, that long

drawn out meals bored him just as much as long drawn out Levées and other Court functions.

It was difficult, therefore, for him to sound enthusiastic when the Prince said:

"I hope, Vivien, that you are dining with me tonight. The Princess is away and I am looking forward not only to entertaining my old cronies at dinner but to finding some amusement later among the glittering lights."

This meant, the Marquis knew, that they would go to some theatrical party which always amused the Prince and they would doubtless end up in one of the Pleasure Houses which would welcome them with open arms.

He told himself almost petulantly that he was too old for such frivolities and so was the Prince.

But His Royal Highness still enjoyed the glitter and tinsel of the stage and the so-called glamour of the 'Ladies of the Town' with the enthusiasm of a young subaltern.

"It sounds delightful, Sire," the Marquis replied.

The Prince chuckled as they walked down the ancient oak stairs of the Palace which had been trodden by Royalty for over four centuries.

A carriage was waiting in the courtyard to convey the Prince the very short distance to Marlborough House.

As he drove away the Marquis and the other Courtiers, Statesmen and Equerries who had seen him off, bowed their heads in the manner due to Royalty then relaxed as the horses carried the Heir to the Throne out of sight.

"Well, that is over," one of the Gentlemen in Waiting said to the Marquis "and now thank God I can get out of this uncomfortable uniform."

"I intend to do the same," the Marquis replied.

He had turned away towards where his own carriage was waiting for him when the Gentleman in Waiting said:

"Oh, by the way, Oakenshaw, I almost forget, the Foreign Secretary asked if you would call to see him at the Foreign Office before luncheon."

"What about?" the Marquis asked in an uncompromising tone.

"I have no idea," was the reply, "but knowing His

Lordship I imagine it will be something he wants done – yesterday.''

The Marquis gave a short laugh with little humour in it.

He was well aware that Lord Rosebery with his ability, his rank and his wealth would have reached power even without the drive and the enquiring brain which made him in many ways, remarkable.

Mr. Gladstone had called him ''The Man of the Future''.

When he was promoted to the post of Foreign Secretary his powers of oratory had won him many admirers and great popularity in the country.

This was accentuated by the fact that his race-horses were superlative and constant winners.

That he included amongst his close friends the much younger Marquis of Oakenshaw was not surprising, for they were both fine sportsmen and both had a sense of humour which enabled them to laugh not only at their contemporaries, but at themselves.

As the Marquis's carriage, which was lightly sprung and drawn by two outstanding horses, drove towards the Foreign Office, he was wondering why Lord Rosebery, with whom he had dined only a few days ago, should wish to see him again in such a hurry.

He would have liked to go back first to his house in Grosvenor Square to change, but if Lord Rosebery said his need of him was urgent then it would obviously be a mistake to keep him waiting.

The horses drew up at the Foreign Office and one of Lord Rosebery's Private Secretaries came hurrying down the steps to greet him, saying as he did so:

''Good morning, My Lord. The Foreign Secretary will be very grateful you were able to come to him so quickly.''

''Good morning Cunningham,'' the Marquis said, having met the young man before. ''What is the excitement?''

''I think His Lordship will want to tell you that himself,'' Mr. Cunningham replied.

He lead the way along the high-ceilinged corridors to open the door of his Chief's office with almost a flourish as he announced:

11

"The Marquis of Oakenshaw, My Lord."

Lord Rosebery gave an exclamation of pleasure and rose to his feet as the Marquis walked towards him.

"Thank you for coming, Vivien," he said. "I must say you look very resplendent. What was the Levée like?"

"Rather more boring than usual," the Marquis replied.

He sat down, as he was expected to do, in a chair opposite the desk as Lord Rosebery resumed his seat and said:

"Thank you for coming. I expect Stanhope told you it was urgent."

"What has happened?" the Marquis enquired. "Has war broken out in Europe, or have the Russians invaded India?"

"Nothing quite as bad as that," Lord Rosebery replied with a smile, "but I want your help in Siam."

"Siam?" the Marquis exclaimed. "I thought the trouble there was settled."

"It is – or soon should be," Lord Rosebery replied, "but at the same time I need you to visit Bangkok on a mission of goodwill."

The Marquis put back his head and laughed.

"I will say one thing for you, Archibald, you are always full of surprises. I might have expected you to ask me to go to Paris or Cairo, but certainly not Siam."

Lord Rosebery settled himself a little more comfortably on the other side of the desk and his eyes were twinkling as he said:

"I am not asking you to put yourself out unduly. I thought perhaps your yacht, which is doubtless gathering barnacles for lack of use, would be a comfortable means of travel, and you could anchor in the river as the French managed to do with their gunboats last year."

"I heard about that," the Marquis answered, "and a nice mess they made of it. I understand that after we had sent a couple of warships into the vicinity everything quietened down."

"It did," Lord Rosebery agreed, "and I might have known, Vivien, you would be well informed."

He was silent for a moment and he looked with a speculative eye on the handsome young man opposite him. Unexpectedly he said:

"With your brain and your knowledge of the world why do you not play a more prominent part in politics? We need you."

The Marquis smiled, which swept the bored look away from his face.

"I think the answer is," he replied, "that those long-winded speeches in the House of Lords are as boring as those who make them."

Lord Rosebery laughed.

"All right, I will not push you into doing anything in Parliament if you will help me, as you have before, outside it."

"Do you really wish me to go to Siam at this particular moment?"

"If it is inconvenient," Lord Rosebery replied, "I am sure I can surmise the reason you are reluctant. Is she very alluring?"

"She is."

He was thinking as he spoke that Lady Bradwell, who had just come into his life, had an allure that he thought and hoped was different from that of anyone he had met before.

The Marquis's love affairs, which were continuous, fiery and passionate, never lasted long because invariably he became bored with the sameness of them.

At the age of 33 he was still unmarried for the simple reason he had not met any woman he could seriously contemplate being in his life indefinitely.

In the majority of his *'affaires de coeur'* there was no question of marriage.

But he found that even the attractive, witty and much acclaimed beauties who came into his life with a flattering eagerness were, as soon as he knew them well, so identical in their outlook and their conversation that all too quickly he began to yawn.

"Good Heavens, Vivien," his closest friend Harry Prestwood had said to him only the week before. "What the hell do you expect out of life? What are you looking for? And if it comes to that, where did Daisy fail you?''

He was speaking of a lady who had been unanimously spoken of as the greatest beauty of the century and who had, like so many women before her, lost her heart and in consequence her head, over the Marquis.

The Countess had a complaisant husband who preferred the country to London, and after ten years of marriage shut his eyes to his wife's private amusements so long as she upheld the dignity of his name in public.

Because of the Marquis's raffish reputation, which would have been more suited to the reign of George IV than that of Queen Victoria for a woman even to be seen with him was enough to start the gossips chattering.

But he had attempted to be very circumspect where Daisy was concerned for the simple reason that he was well aware that since they were both notable people from the public point of view, their association if noticed, was bound to be sensational.

But Daisy fell obviously in love and they began to be talked about. So because the Marquis disliked the innuendos of his friends and the snide remarks of the gossip columnists, he brought the affairs to an abrupt end.

When he wished he could be very ruthless and very determined. Once he had made up his mind, no amount of tears, pleading or recriminations would alter it.

''How could you do this to me?'' Daisy cried, when he told her he thought it best that they should not see so much of each other.

''I am afraid there is nothing else we can do,'' the Marquis replied.

''I love you,'' Daisy said, ''I adore you. I never thought it possible I could love a man as I love you.''

''You are certainly very flattering,'' the Marquis answered, ''but you cannot afford to damage your reputation either in public or at Marlborough House.''

Daisy had stiffened and for a moment her blue eyes were swimming with tears as she looked at the Marquis incredulously as if she doubted he was speaking the truth.

''What do you mean about Marlborough House?'' she

enquired. "The Prince would never say anything against me, as you well know."

"Last night at dinner the Princess asked me very pointedly," the Marquis replied, "when your husband was returning to London."

Daisy was silent.

She was well aware that to antagonise the Princess would be disastrous socially, and though she thought it unlikely that the beautiful Alexandra would become an enemy, she had never been as friendly as Daisy would have liked.

As if he knew he had scored an important point, the Marquis said quietly:

"I want to thank you, Daisy, for the happiness you have given me, and I hope we shall always be friends."

As he spoke he knew he sounded pompous, but there was nothing else he could do.

The truth was he was not so concerned with Daisy's reputation as with the fact that she no longer attracted him as she had at first.

He could not understand why all too quickly every woman in whom he was interested seemed after a very short time to repeat and re-repeat what she said until he could anticipate almost every word before it passed her lips.

He did not wish a woman to be too clever – God forbid. Nothing was more infuriating than a blue stocking.

But at the same time even while Daisy could set his body on fire, as far as his mind was concerned he criticised the banality of what she said even when the words were spoken through her perfectly curved cupid-bow lips.

"Damn it all," he had said to Harry, not once but a dozen times, "I shall never marry."

"Of course you will," Harry replied. "You must have an heir, and quite frankly the Castle would benefit by having a hostess at the end of the table."

If Harry had exploded a bomb under his feet, the Marquis could not have been more surprised.

"Are you insinuating," he asked, "that I am not a good host?"

"No-one could be a better one," Harry answered, "but

at the same time when you are entertaining – and no-one does it more lavishly – it seems somehow unbalanced that there is not at the other end of the table a beautiful woman wearing the Oakenshaw diamonds, which she would also wear at the Opening of Parliament.''

The Marquis had thrown back his head and laughed.

''You talk exactly like my mother,'' he said.

At the same time he knew that Harry was right.

It was expected and inevitable that eventually he should take a wife to be hostess in the Castle, in London and in his other houses in different parts of the country, besides taking her hereditary place beside him at Court.

Then he thought of the boredom he would endure if he had to listen to the platitudes mouthed by some young girl at breakfast, hear them again at luncheon and at dinner, with the terrifying knowledge that they would continue ad infinitum for the rest of his life.

''I cannot and WILL not do it,'' he told himself.

Having disposed of Daisy very effectively and softened the blow in his usual generous manner with an extremely expensive present from Cartiers, he had looked round for someone else to please his eye.

There had been no-one until last week when, attending a dinner-party given by a Member of the Government whom he usually ignored, he found himself sitting next to a woman he had never seen before, called Lady Bradwell.

She was beautiful, it went without saying, otherwise he was quite certain she would not have been put next to him.

But she was rather unusual in that her beauty had not been seen by or appreciated before by the Marlborough House Set.

''Where have you been hiding?'' the Marquis enquired.

''I have been in Paris,'' she replied, ''and in mourning for a year.''

''That accounts for it.''

He meant that it accounted not only for his not having met her before, but also for the extremely elegant way in which she was dressed, the manner in which she spoke and parried his bolder advances with an expertise which most English women lacked.

By the time dinner was over the Marquis was definitely intrigued.

Two days later he settled himself down to a chase which he knew of old would not take long nor was there any question of the outcome.

The Marquis was not particularly conceited, but he would have been extremely stupid if he had not been aware that any woman on whom he set his sights was invariably and instantly ready to comply with his demands, only making a token resistence to salve her pride.

Lady Bradwell, however, had not only intrigued him but contrived with what he thought was unexpected cleverness to keep him guessing.

In simple words, the Marquis had not yet reached his objective, and although it was a foregone conclusion he had no wish to go abroad at this particular moment.

It suddenly struck him that as Lady Bradwell had no husband, there would be no difficulty in persuading her – discreetly chaperoned of course – to come with him.

Aloud he asked:

"When do you wish me to set off on what you call a goodwill mission, Archibald? What exactly am I expected to do?"

He saw by the smile on the Foreign Secretary's face and the twinkle in his eyes, that Lord Rosebery was not only delighted at his acquiescence but guessed more or less the reason for it.

"The answer to your first question is as soon as possible," he said. "As for your second, since you know what has been happening in Siam I will not explain that you will be going to soothe the King's apprehension over the Anglo-French agreement of last year."

He smiled as he continued:

"You must make His Majesty believe that it will not be detrimental to his country but will actually ensure its independence."

"What you are saying," the Marquis remarked, "is that the Colonial Powers, the British in Burma and the French in Laos, will treat Siam as a buffer state."

"Exactly," the Foreign Secretary agreed, "but after all the disagreeableness that has been – especially from the French – King Chulalongkorn is naturally nervous and apprehensive as to the future."

"I hope he will not be that," the Marquis remarked. "I have always agreed with you that Chulalongkorn is one of the great Kings of this age and will certainly go down in history."

The Foreign Secretary nodded.

Both men were thinking how the King had begun his reign by proclaiming that the children born to slaves were to be free men and had gradually been freeing his subjects from slavery ever since.

He had introduced a modern postal system, built railroads and replaced regional feudal Barons who were far too powerful by centrally appointed Governors accountable directly to the throne.

When the Marquis had visited Siam some years previously he had been tremendously impressed by the King and his reforms especially when His Majesty had said to him personally:

"All children from my own to the poorest shall have an equal chance of education."

King Chulalongkorn was determined that Siam should not be simply a Westernised dependency and one of the ways to avoid it was to pay for their own path towards progress.

At the same time, with Great Britain in full control of Burma he was anxious about the growing power and influence of the French in Indo-China.

Last year there had been trouble and two French gunboats on entering the Chiapana River to go up to Bangkok, had fired at the Thai forts.

There were casualties on both sides, but by now all the animosity should have died down.

"What I want you to do," the Foreign Secretary said, "is to make the King aware that Britain is genuinely anxious to be friendly and I know no-one, Vivien, who can do this better than yourself."

"You are being very flattering," the Marquis said, "but I am well aware you are doing so in order to get your own way."

He sighed.

"All right, I will go, but only if I can be sure I can take an amusing party with me."

"What you are telling me," Lord Rosebery remarked, "is that it depends on the object of your vacillating heart at this particular moment accepting your invitation."

He paused before he added;

"I have quite a long acquaintance with you, Vivien, and I have never yet known any woman refuse you."

"There always has to be a first time."

"Make sure it is not now."

Lord Rosebery rose to his feet adding:

"I have a meeting which is waiting for me. Can you have luncheon with me tomorrow? I can then tell you more about the position in Siam and also give you letters to the King and to our Minister and Consul General in Bangkok, Captain Henry Michael Jones, who is a V.C."

"I have an uncomfortable feeling you have pressurised me into this," the Marquis answered. "If anything goes wrong, Archibald, I swear this is the last time I shall agree to one of your propositions which when you were Foreign Secretary before, took me to parts of the world I had no particular wish to visit."

"Nonsense!" Lord Rosebery replied. "You know as well as I do you will enjoy getting away from the intrigues at Marlborough House and the long drawn out meals, at which I have often seen you fidgetting. And who knows – in pastures new you may find the rare orchid, or is it the star, for which you are always searching."

The Marquis stared at him incredulously.

"Who said I was searching for anything?"

"Of course you are," Lord Rosebery replied. "And with your looks, Vivien, your position and wealth you have everything, except what is more important to a man than anything else."

"What is that?" the Marquis asked in a hostile voice,

well aware of the answer.

"Love," Lord Rosebery replied.

The Marquis was just about to say that that was the last thing he wanted and could do well without it, when he remembered that Lord Rosebery had lost his wife only four years ago and his friends were aware he had been a lonely and unhappy man ever since.

He therefore changed his mind about what he had been about to say, and merely remarked lightly:

"I have always been told that 'he travels fastest who travels alone'."

"A somewhat trite remark for you, Vivien," Lord Rosebery dryly, "though naturally it depends where you are going."

The Marquis appreciated the subtlety of the remark, knowing that the Foreign Secretary had often begged him to use his unusual and brilliant gifts in a much more serious way than he was doing at the moment.

There was a brief silence before the Foreign Secretary said:

"When you return I have a more serious proposition to discuss with you."

The Marquis raised his eyebrows and asked:

"What can that be?"

"I am not going to tell you about it now," Lord Rosebery replied, "but I have already mentioned it to Her Majesty who is very pleased with the idea."

"I presume," the Marquis said slowly, "you are thinking of a Governorship?"

"Perhaps something higher. Anyway hurry back – I do not want you away in the wilds too long."

The Marquis rose to his feet.

"I will have luncheon with you tomorrow, Archibald," he said, "and you had better convince me then that my journey is really necessary, or I swear to you I will cry off at the last moment."

"You have never failed me yet," the Foreign Secretary replied, "and actually I only wish I had the time to come with you. If I had, I should not hesitate to set out on a cruise which may or may not lead you to your Golden Fleece.''

As they walked towards the door, Lord Rosebery put his hand on the younger man's shoulder.

"I am quite certain, Vivien, she will accept your invitation eagerly – in fact too eagerly! But let us hope that she will at least keep you amused until your return."

"Your impertinence astounds me!'' the Marquis exclaimed.

Both men were laughing as they stepped out of the Foreign Secretary's office into the corridor.

. . . .

Tarina Worthington rang the bell of 115 Belgrave Square and waited a little nervously until it was opened by a footman in livery.

A Butler came forward from the back of the hall as she asked:

"I have called to see Lady Bradwell."

"Have you an appointment, Madam?"

"I am afraid not," Tarina answered, "but will you tell her that her cousin, Miss Tarina Worthington, wishes to see her.''

"Of course, Miss.''

The Butler's almost hostile manner changed when Tarina said the word "cousin", and he walked slowly towards the Morning Room and opened the door for her to pass inside.

"I will inform Her Ladyship you are here, Miss," he said.

Tarina looked around at the square, high-ceilinged room which was furnished in a manner which proclaimed opulence rather than good taste, and caught sight of herself in a large mirror.

As she did so, she was aware of why the Butler had at first been ready to turn her away rather than permit her to enter the house.

The black dress she had bought after her father died had been very cheap and in the winter sunshine it looked shabby.

Her coat, which unfortunately was indispensable with the temperature only a little above freezing, was threadbare and had been her mother's for many years.

She told herself with a sad little smile that her appearance was a disaster.

She just had not dared to spend much money on mourning, when all that stood between her and starvation was the very small sum of money which was left in the bank after her father's funeral.

"How could Papa ever save?" Tarina asked herself despairingly.

She had known before she had sold everything that was hers in the Vicarage that she would not get more than a few pounds for it.

Because she felt nervous at visiting her cousin whom she had not seen for two years, she tried to arrange her hat at a more becoming angle.

She was aware that because she had not had the time to wash her hair for the last week, it had lost some of the red sparkle that her mother had always told her came from an Austrian ancestress.

"It is funny, Tarina," she said, "but the strain of red hair of the Viennese which has always been so much admired will skip perhaps two generations in my family and then reappear."

"Was my great-grandmother very beautiful?" Tarina had asked.

"So I have always heard," her mother replied, "and also extremely talented. She had a splendid voice and her diaries tell us that she was greatly in demand at parties in Vienna. On two occasions she sang at the Schönbrunn Palace in front of the Emperor Franz Joseph and Empress Elizabeth, who also had red hair."

"Do you think I would have a good voice – if it was trained?" Tarina asked.

Her mother smiled.

"I have no idea, my darling," she answered. "You sing delightfully in Church, but you and I know that is not the same as being able to hold an audience spellbound."

She paused before she went on:

"But there is one thing you can be quite certain of, and that is that Papa and I have to scrimp and save to pay the lessons you are having at the moment, and we certainly cannot afford to pay for any more."

What Tarina did know about her red hair was that when she was happy the colour of it seemed to glow, but when she was unwell or worried the red faded and her head looked dull as if it reflected the feelings of her mind and heart.

Now there was only a touch of red to be seen, but her skin was dazzlingly white as it always was, and in the sunshine it had almost a translucent quality about it.

Her eyes, which were sometimes green and sometimes grey, seemed at the moment only dark with anxiety and worry.

"Supposing Cousin Betty . . refuses me?" she whispered to herself. "What . . shall I . . do? Where . . shall I go?"

The door opened.

"Her Ladyship will see you, Miss," the Butler announced.

"Thank you," Tarina replied.

She followed him across the hall and up the staircase to a wide landing.

Here through an open door she could see a huge Reception Room with imitation Louis XIV chairs and sofas, a carpet in a dull colour and several rather austere chandeliers.

But she had only time for a quick glance before the Butler walked on.

At the end of a corridor he opened a door into what Tarina knew was a Boudoir.

It was something which her mother had described to her and she had always longed to see. There was no mistaking that this was one, with pale blue curtains and a chaise longue in the same brocade.

It gave the impression of exquisite femininity which was augmented by the huge vases of Malmaison carnations which not only scented the room but were reflected and re-reflected in the gold-framed mirrors which hung on the walls.

The room was empty and even as Tarina looked around,

someone came through another door at the far end of it.

With a little murmur she moved forward and as she did so, the woman who had entered exclaimed:

"Tarina! I could hardly believe it was you! What are you doing in London?"

Tarina reached her side.

"Oh Betty . . it is kind of you to see me."

"Of course I want to see you," Lady Bradwell answered.

Then she paused in consternation.

"But you are in black! Why?"

"Papa died a month ago."

"Oh, I am sorry! I had no idea, Dearest. You will miss him."

"More than I can tell you. But now he is dead you will understand I have to earn my own living."

"You poor child!" Lady Bradwell exclaimed. "Come and sit down and tell me all about it."

She arranged herself in the corner of the sofa and Tarina sat down beside her.

As she did so, she thought no-one could be lovelier than her Cousin Betty.

With her fair hair and love-in-the-mist blue eyes, she was like a painting by Fragonard and Tarina could only stare at her wide-eyed.

"You are beautiful, Betty! Much more beautiful than you used to be! And there is something else different about you."

Lady Bradwell smiled.

"That is what everyone says, and it is because I have been in Paris. Oh, Tarina, I am so lucky! After my husband died I was invited to stay with one of his relatives who had always been kind to me."

"I was very sorry to hear about your husband," Tarina said. "I know Papa wrote to you."

"He wrote me a beautiful letter," Lady Bradwell answered, "but as I can be frank with you – I was not unhappy at becoming a widow."

Tarina gave an exclamation.

"Oh, Betty! Why not?"

Lady Bradwell gave a little sigh.

"My husband was ill all the last year of our marriage and it was very, very dull looking after him. And even before that he was very crotchety. After all, he was forty years older than I was."

"I know," Tarina said. "But everyone said it was such a brilliant marriage as he was a very important man."

"I suppose he was kind in his own way," Betty replied, "but at the same time, Tarina, though I enjoyed going to the dinner-parties and balls, we were always entertaining Arthur's friends, who also were old. I did not really have much fun until now."

She gave a little cry and said:

"I cannot tell you how wonderful it is to be here in London! To be on my own, to be able to afford to live in this house, and have the most glorious, marvellous clothes!"

"And lots and lots of friends to admire you," Tarina said.

"But of course," Betty replied. "I am acclaimed as a beauty and Tarina, what do you think . . ."

It was just like the old days when Betty, being the older, had talked and Tarina had listened.

Now as Tarina sat with her eyes on her cousin's face, apparently spell-bound, Betty was talking as she had when she was seventeen and supposed to be grown up, while Tarina at fifteen was still in a way a child.

"What has happened?" Tarina asked as Betty paused.

"I have been asked," Betty said slowly, "to go on a cruise – in a yacht with the Marquis of Oakenshaw."

"In a yacht?" Tarina exclaimed. "Are you a good sailor?"

"That is immaterial," Betty said quickly. "He is the most acclaimed, the most handsome, the most elusive man in London, and I think he is pursuing me."

"How thrilling! How exciting!" Tarina exclaimed. "Will he ask you to marry him?"

Betty gave a little laugh.

"I think that is very unlikely. He is an avowed bachelor – as all the women have hastened to tell me."

Tarina looked puzzled.

"I do not understand . . ."

25

Betty glanced at her and then said quickly:

"Of course I may persuade him to change his mind, but in the meantime I shall be his guest and every other woman who has ever known him will die of envy!"

Tarina wondered why that should be so satisfactory, but at the same time because she loved her cousin, she said:

"I am thrilled for you. What are you leaving?"

"Almost immediately – in two day's time. Tarina, I do not know how I shall ever be ready!"

Tarina smiled.

"I am sure you will have plenty of people to help you."

"I ought to have new clothes, although that will be impossible in the time. Thank goodness I have brought some glorious gowns from Paris. I spent a fortune on them!"

Tarina looked at the dress that Betty was wearing at the moment and seeing the richness of the silk from which it was made and the real lace which trimmed it, she knew that what it cost would keep her in comfort for a year at least.

She thrust such thoughts away from her mind and said:

"I came here, Betty, not to be a nuisance, but just to ask you . . if you would help me by giving me a . . reference."

"A reference?"

The astonishment in Betty's voice made Tarina smile.

"Dearest, you must be aware that Papa had no money of his own when he was alive apart from his small stipend, and now he is dead, I have to earn my living."

"Oh, Tarina, I am sorry!" Betty exclaimed. "How terrible for you! What are you going to do?"

"I shall be a governess," Tarina said quietly. "There is nothing else for which I am qualified. I expect I shall have to be a nursery governess to start with because I am so young."

"You mean you will have to waste your brain, which your father always said was as good as a boy's, on a lot of squalling children?" Betty asked. "Tarina, it is not fair!"

"I will manage," Tarina answered. "But as you know, Betty, I shall never get into a decent place unless I have a really excellent reference, and there is no-one I can ask except you."

"My dear, I will write you a eulogy which will make

everyone want to engage you immediately!''

"Thank you," Tarina said in relief.

"But first I want to show you my gowns," Betty went on, "which have 'Paris' written all over them, and also the new wardrobe I have bought especially to hold them."

She rose as she spoke and Tarina followed her into the adjoining Bedroom which was even more impressive than the Boudoir.

There was a large bed draped with silk curtains held at the sides with carved gold angels.

At the foot of it over a spread of real lace, there was an ermine cover. The pillows had frills of the same lace threaded through with blue satin ribbon and a large monogram embroidered in the centre of them.

Tarina looked around in astonishment. She had often tried to imagine the type of bedroom that fashionable ladies would have in their large houses, but she had never thought of anything so luxurious or so pretty.

"I have redecorated this room and the Boudoir," Betty said. "I have now started on the Drawing-Room, which is heavy and ponderous rather like my husband."

She glanced at her cousin mischievously under her eyelashes as she spoke, and Tarina who knew she was trying to shock her, exclaimed:

"Betty! You should not say such things!"

"It is true. Oh, Tarina, it is such a relief to be free of him! He always talked to me as if I were an imbecile, and after our honeymoon, which was pretty horrible, he never even paid me a compliment."

The pain in her voice was so evident that impulsively Tarina put her arm round her saying:

"Never mind, Dearest. You are so beautiful I am sure the Marquis will want to marry you. Or perhaps you will meet an alluring Prince and reign over one of those delightful little countries in Europe I am always reading about in the newspapers."

Betty laughed.

"You are making it into a Fairy Story!"

"That is what you should be – a Fairy Princess," Tarina

27

said, "and you certainly look like one."

"Only because my Fairy Godmother – or rather the *Comtesse* helped me by buying exactly what Cinderella would wear. There are some of my gowns in this wardrobe and a whole room full of them next door."

She walked towards the wardrobe that was painted blue and white to match the walls of the room which the mirrors reflected and re-reflected the furniture and the sunshine coming through the windows.

She put out her hand towards it as she did so there was a knock which made her glance towards the door of the corridor.

"Who is it?" she asked.

"It's me, M'Lady."

"Come in, Bates."

The Butler who had looked after Tarina downstairs stood in the doorway.

"Excuse me, M'Lady, but I've bad news."

"Bad news?" Betty questioned. "What is it?"

"Jones, M'Lady. She's had an accident."

"How . . how could she? What has happened?"

"She was getting something out of the large cupboard on the top landing, M'Lady," Bates explained, "and because what she was trying to lift down was heavy, she over-balanced and fell off the steps."

"Good Heavens!" Betty exclaimed. "Is she hurt?"

"I'm afraid, M'Lady, she's broken her leg."

Betty gave a little cry.

"Broken her leg? How can she have? Oh, poor Jones, I am so sorry for her!"

She paused then she added almost beneath her breath:

"But what on earth am I to do without her?"

CHAPTER TWO

With an effort Betty said to the Butler:

"Tell Jones I will come up and see her later. I suppose the Doctor has done what he can for her?"

"He's set her leg, M'Lady, an' said he'll come back tomorrow, I think Jones is sleeping now."

"That is the best thing she can do," Betty replied, "and I would like tea in the *Boudoir* in about half-an-hour for Miss Worthington and myself."

"Very good, M'Lady."

The Butler bowed and left the room.

Betty looked at Tarina with consternation in her eyes.

"Can you imagine anything more terrible," she exclaimed, "than that my lady's-maid should let me down at this moment? I shall have to try to find somebody else, although I am sure it is an impossibility."

She paused. Then she went on:

"There is the packing to finish, although Jones has done most of it. But how can I engage a maid in such a hurry without having any idea how she will look after my clothes and do my hair?"

She looked towards the wardrobes as if she expected they would be able to help her.

Then Tarina said:

"I could pack for you, if that would be of any help."

"Actually I suppose the house-maids could do that," Betty replied.

Then she turned towards her cousin with a new expression in her eyes.

"Tarina!" she exclaimed. "You used to do my hair before

29

I married, and you can sew better than anybody I know."

Tarina drew in her breath as if she could hardly believe what she guessed her cousin was about to say.

Then hesitatingly, as if she was afraid she would offend Tarina, Betty asked:

"Would you? Would you come with me, or is it too much to ask?"

"Come with you on the yacht?" Tarina enquired.

"That is what I am saying," Betty replied, "but I could not ask the Marquis to invite you as an extra guest."

"No, of course not!" Tarina exclaimed. "But if you want me to, I will come as your lady's-maid, or in any other capacity."

Betty's eyes lightened. Then she said:

"It is the sort of kind thing you would say, Tarina, but I feel it is too much to ask! At the same time you are looking for employment."

"Of course I am," Tarina said, "and that is why I am here. I can imagine nothing more exciting than to be employed by you, and to go abroad!"

Betty sat down on a chair in front of the fireplace, and put her fingers up to her forehead.

"Let us work this out," she said. "Remember, Tarina, I am desperate – really desperate!"

"Of course you are, and you must look your best to fascinate the Marquis."

Tarina thought as she spoke that it would be difficult for any man not to be fascinated by her cousin.

Even though she was so worried, Betty was looking exceedingly beautiful.

Her hair picked up the sunshine so that she seemed to be a poem in pink, white and gold, and more like a Fragonard picture than ever.

"You will have to tell me exactly what a lady's-maid does," Tarina said, "when she is not looking after you. I am sure it cannot be very difficult."

"If it were here in the house it would be," Betty replied, "because it would not be easy to hoodwink the other

30

servants. But when I said I wanted to bring Jones with me the Marquis agreed.''

She paused before she added:

''I am almost certain he said that the other Ladies would not be accompanied by their maids because they hated the sea.''

Tarina laughed.

''I am sure that is true. I remember years ago your mother saying that Ashton, her maid, absolutely refused to go to Paris with her.''

''That is true,'' Betty exclaimed, ''and although Mama complained it was an inconvenience, it was really quite a relief to be without her.''

''I think all servants hate change and moving about.''

''That is why I employ a French woman. They are much more mobile.''

''French?''

Betty laughed.

''You are surprised because we call her 'Jones'. Actually her name is 'Janzé', but you can imagine what the household made of that! They started to call her 'Jonesy', and it was more than I could bear, so in the end I said she should be addressed as 'Jones'.''

Tarina chuckled.

''That was certainly sensible, if misleading.''

''You will be 'Janzé','' Betty said, ''and as your French is very much better than mine, no one will be in the least suspicious. It will also account for the fact that you do not look like an English servant.''

''I hope not!'' Tarina exclaimed.

They both laughed. Then after a moment Betty said more seriously:

''You are quite certain dearest, that you do not mind my asking this of you?''

''Mind?'' Tarina gasped. ''I am absolutely delighted! I think my Guardian Angel must have brought me to you at exactly the right moment.''

She saw Betty was about to say something and added quickly:

"Let us be practical and get down to work. Tell me exactly what you want me to do."

"There is another trunk to be packed," Betty replied, "and the house-maids can help with that. In the meantime, you must not tell them you are coming with me as a lady's-maid, but merely accompanying me as the Marquis's guest."

There was a little pause. Then Tarina said hesitatingly:

"They will hardly believe that when they look at me. Could you . . give me perhaps just a . . little money, Betty, not much . . but enough for me to buy something suitable in black as befits my position?"

"Just one . . .?" Betty questioned, then stopped.

As if for the first time, she looked at what her cousin was wearing beneath the shabby coat and exclaimed:

"Oh, Tarina, how selfish of me not to have sent you some clothes before now! I never thought of doing such a thing, and I have masses of discarded gowns and . . ."

She stopped suddenly, and gave an exclamation which was almost a cry.

"You are in mourning!" she said as if it was a new discovery, "and I have the perfect answer for that."

Tarina looked at her wide-eyed.

"I have been wearing mourning," Betty said, "for a year. You know what the French are like about death, so conventional that they look like crows up to the very last hour of the very last day of a year after their relatives departed this world."

The way Betty spoke made Tarina give a little chuckle as if she could not help herself.

"But I cheated towards the end," Betty went on, "with gowns of pale mauve and white which will be perfect for you if it is hot in Siam while the black ones are eminently suitable for a lady's-maid who, if she is French, would look *chic* even in sack-cloth!"

Tarina gave a laugh and said incredulously:

"I do not believe it! You are making all this up! It sounds exactly like a fairy-tale!"

"That is what I hope it will be," Betty said, "but I assure

you there are two trunks of black clothes which I brought back with me from Paris, meaning to send most of the gowns to a charity. I know, dearest, that you will look lovely in them."

"That is the last thing a lady's-maid should look," Tarina said sternly.

"The cruise will not last for ever," Betty replied, "and when we come back, you will find employment in some very grand house where you will doubtless captivate the oldest son, marry him, and live happily ever afterwards."

"I think that is unlikely," Tarina said. "At the same time, I should be thrilled, very, very thrilled to have even one new gown in which I need not be ashamed of my appearance."

"I will give you all my mourning clothes," Betty said, "and never again, my dearest little cousin, will I be so selfish as not to give you every gown I no longer want. So if nothing else, you will be the best-dressed Governess in the whole of England!"

As she spoke she thought perhaps that would be a great mistake!

It might not be only the oldest son of the house who was pursuing Tarina, but perhaps the father of the children she was teaching, with disastrous results.

Then she told herself that was a bridge they would cross later. All that mattered for the moment was that Tarina would look after her on the yacht and make sure that she looked her best and most alluring for the Marquis.

Tarina rose from where she was sitting to take off her coat and bonnet, and put them on a chair which stood against a wall.

"The first thing I must do," she said, "is look to see how Jones does your hair before it gets untidy. It is a long time since I arranged it for you, and I like the new way you are wearing it."

It was in fact, very attractive, being swept back from Betty's oval forehead and arranged in a small knot on the top of her head, with at the same time, a very soft golden fringe which seemed somehow to intensify the blue of her eyes.

Tarina walked behind her as she sat on the sofa, then round to the front before she said:

"I am sure I can do it just like that."

Betty gave a little sigh of relief.

"You always were clever with your fingers. Do you remember when we used to dress up and act a play at Christmas for Papa and Mama? You were author, producer, wardrobe-mistress, and actually you were a far better actress then I was."

"But you only had to look beautiful!" Tarina said. "At least I should be able to act the part of a lady's-maid without much difficulty. Do I curtsy to you?"

Betty laughed.

"Jones is far too grand to do that, but she used to make a small bob, with reluctance, to my husband, and the *Comtesse*. So I imagine, if you do come in contact with the Marquis or any other of his distinguished guests, you curtsy to them."

Tarina considered this for a moment. Then she said:

"I think it would be a good idea to have my meals in my own cabin."

"I will arrange that," Betty said. "I expect it is quite the usual thing to do, as I am sure Jones would think it beneath her to eat with the crew."

"She sounds frightening! Why do you have somebody like that as your lady's-maid?"

"Because she is a marvellous maid, and even the *Comtesse* approved of her. She was going to find me a French maid to replace anybody I brought with me from England."

"I only hope I shall give satisfaction . . M'Lady!" Tarina said humbly.

Then they both laughed.

"It is going to be such fun to have you with me," Betty said. "Between ourselves, Tarina, I am rather overcome by the Marquis, who is definitely frightening, and although I have met some very charming people in Paris, it is not the same as moving in the stuck-up Marlborough House Set."

"Are they stuck up?" Tarina asked.

"They 'look down their noses' at everybody except themselves," Betty replied, "and are very, very conscious of their own importance."

"Who are the other guests?"

34

"I do not really know," Betty answered, "but I think they will be old friends who you may be certain will not bore the Marquis. Everybody tells me he is very easily bored."

"He certainly sounds rather frightening," Tarina answered. "Are you quite certain you will enjoy being with him?"

"Of course! That is much more important than his feelings."

Betty gave a little cry.

"That is *lèse-majesté*! The Marquis is the most important bachelor in the whole of Society, and women run after him in the most outrageous fashion."

She paused before she went on reminiscently:

"I saw the beautiful Lady de Grey positively fawning over him the other night, and so was her rival the Marchioness of Londonderry. If they had not been Ladies of Quality, they would have been fighting over him like two fish-wives!"

Tarina looked puzzled.

"B.but I thought . . Lady de Grey . . and the Marchioness were married!"

She was thinking as she spoke that she had seen pictures of them in *'The Ladies Journal'*.

It was a magazine which her mother had taken when she was alive, and which after her death she was sometimes lent by ladies in the Parish.

There was a little silence. Then as Betty realised how innocent and unworldly her cousin was, she said in a different tone of voice:

"Come along, Tarina. We cannot sit here gossiping when we have so much to do. I am going to call Robinson who is my head house-maid."

She hesitated a moment then said:

"I will tell her that you are going to assist me to sort out the gowns which still have to be packed, then she and the other house-maids can put them into the trunk."

"That is a good idea," Tarina agreed.

"In the meantime, I will tell Newman the Butler that you are staying here, and to bring up your baggage."

"I am afraid I did not bring it to the house with me."

35

"Then where is it?" Betty enquired. "Or have you left it in the country?"

"I brought everything I possess to London," Tarina replied. "I was planning that if you gave me a reference I would go at once to a Domestic Bureau in Mount Street, which I was told is the best place."

"That will not be necessary now," Betty interrupted.

"So I left my luggage," Tarina went on, "although there is not a great deal of it, at Paddington Station."

"I will send a footman to collect it."

Betty walked from the bedroom into the *Boudoir* where a Butler and two footmen were setting a tea-table.

There was an enormous amount of silver which looked to Tarina very opulent, and so many plates of sandwiches and cakes of every description that they made her feel hungry.

She had left the Vicarage, into which the new incumbent would move today, at six o'clock in the morning, caught a train at the nearest station, and come straight to Belgrave Square to call on her cousin without waiting to have anything to eat.

Almost as if she sensed what she was thinking Betty said:

"I am sure you must be hungry after such a long day. I should have thought of it before."

Without waiting for Tarina's reply she said to the Butler:

"Bring up a boiled egg for Miss Worthington's tea, and inform Mrs. Peel that she will be staying here with me tonight. Also send James or Frank to Paddington Station to collect her trunk from the Left-Luggage Office."

"Very good, M'Lady."

As the Butler left the room followed by the two footmen, Tarina said:

"I have come to the conclusion that I am dreaming! I was so afraid when I came here that you might refuse to see me, and actually I was quite frightened that I would not find anywhere to sleep the night."

Betty put out her hand and laid it on Tarina's arm.

"I am so sorry to know of your father's death," she said, "for you must know how much I admired Uncle David. If I had known, I would have worried as to what would happen to you."

"Now you are being so kind, I can hardly believe that I have not walked straight into a fairy-story."

"Whatever happens in the future," Betty said firmly, "you can rely on me. I have never forgotten how kind Aunt Louise was to me when my mother died, and actually, as you know, I have always thought of you as if you were my sister."

"You are a very beautiful and very kind . . sister," Tarina said with a little sob in her voice.

Betty pressed her hand. Then she said:

"Stop making me feel sentimental. If I cry, it will make my eye-lashes run."

Tarina looked at her in sheer astonishment.

"Your eye-lashes?"

"Do not be so foolish, Tarina! You know I never had dark eye-lashes in the past. Nobody must know, but I tint them very, very carefully with a hair-dye."

"It is certainly very effective, and very well done."

"It has to be," Betty replied, "because it is considered very fast for any Lady to make up her face. But I can assure you they all use face-powder when nobody is looking, and rub rouge into their cheeks and on their lips."

She smiled as she went on:

"When I first realised it was necessary I used to rub geranium petals on my mouth, but now I go to a Theatrical Costumier who sells grease-paint and other cosmetics to actresses."

Tarina looked at Betty's face closely. Then she said:

"You always had the most beautiful skin and your face does not look very different to me."

"Wait until you see me in the morning after I have been dancing all night!"

They laughed and Tarina said:

"Your secrets are safe with me, and I am sure it would be a great mistake for anybody else to be aware of them, especially the Marquis."

There was a little pause as if Betty considered this. Then she said:

"As the Marquis has always associated with sophisticated and very beautiful women who are much older than I am, I should be surprised if he is not well aware of the difference between an orchid and a daisy."

"If you are comparing yourself with a daisy," Tarina said, "I do not think it is at all a good simile. You look just like a pale pink rose, very lovely, and perfection in itself! That is how he must always think of you."

"He is not only critical, but blasé," Betty said, "and we have to think of ways to interest and amuse him. You know, Tarina, you are much cleverer at that sort of thing than I am."

Tarina began to think that the Marquis sounded a spoiled, rather unpleasant person, and she wondered why Betty was so interested in him.

However, having met Lord Bradwell, whom her cousin had married, she could quite understand that he was not only too old, but too pompous and in her opinion too boring to make any girl as young and as sweet-natured as Betty, happy.

"Why did she marry that old man?" she had asked her father when Betty had gone off on her honeymoon looking exquisitely lovely, and at the same time young enough to be her husband's grandchild.

The Vicar who was a handsome man, had sighed.

"I can only hope they will be happy, my darling," he had answered. "The flesh-pots of Egypt have an irresistible allure, and the primrose path in life is often prickly, and at times painful."

Tarina, who had understood exactly what he was saying had answered with a sigh:

"I do so want Betty to be happy."

"So do I," the Vicar agreed, "but if she had been my daughter, I would have insisted on a long engagement instead of pushing her up the aisle in what I consider an indecent speed before she had time to realise exactly what marriage entailed."

There was no doubt, Tarina thought looking back, that Betty's father and her mother, who was her Aunt Alice, although they lived in a large house and owned a great deal of land, were not actually very wealthy.

They had therefore been thrilled that their only child should marry the Lord Lieutenant of the County, who was of great importance socially and also extremely rich.

"Betty will have everything – but everything!" Tarina's Aunt had said to her.

It was only later when Tarina saw Betty after she had returned from her honeymoon that she realised she was not happy, and that her husband's position of importance did not compensate for his shortcomings as a man.

Now she said impulsively:

"Darling Betty, you are so kind to me. I promise you I will do everything in my power to make you happy in the future."

"I am happy," Betty replied. "It is wonderful, Tarina, to have so much money and nobody to complain about how I spend it."

Tarina would have replied that money would not make her as happy as if she had love.

Then she thought that was too intimate a thing to say, but she thought that if the Marquis was playing fast and loose with Betty's affections, then she would want to murder him.

No one knew better than she did that Betty not only had a sweet nature, but was also in many ways very vulnerable.

She was impulsive and gave people her affection almost before she knew them, and Tarina had thought at times she was very easily taken in.

It struck her now that the Marquis sounded too sophisticated and too overpowering for somebody like her cousin, and was not the sort of person she should marry.

She used to envisage when they were very young that Betty would marry a charming young Country Squire. They would hunt and take part in all the County interests, and find a mutual happiness in such simple pursuits.

Looking at Betty, she thought now it was inevitable because she was so lovely that she would be a success in London.

Although she knew nothing about what happened in what was called 'The Marlborough House Set', she would have been deaf if she had not heard, even in the small Parish where she lived, people talking about the Prince of Wales.

There was endless gossip about his infatuations for acknowledged Beauties like Lily Langtry, Lady Brooke, and now Mrs. Keppel.

There were also whispers about the times when he went to Paris alone, when Princess Alexandra was in Denmark visiting her own family.

A great deal of what was said had been incomprehensible even when the gossips had raised their voices loud enough for Tarina to hear, but she still knew it was improper behaviour on his part, not only as Heir to the Throne, but also as a married man.

She had however, not been particularly interested because she had thought it very unlikely that she would ever come in contact with such people.

It had never occurred to her that Betty, who she loved, would do so.

Now she could understand how such notable persons would have a fascination for a young woman who had nursed a querulous, disagreeable old husband until he died, and then had lived abroad in the strictly conventional society of the aristocratic French.

Tarina finished her tea, having consumed not only an egg, but also a number of sandwiches and delicious little cakes of which there seemed to be an inordinate amount, while she listened to Betty.

Almost as if it had been pent up inside her because she had nobody in whom she could confide, she told Tarina of her astonishing success at the very first Ball she had attended after her return to London.

From that moment invitations had poured in until incredibly quickly for somebody unknown she had been invited to a party at Marlborough House.

"The Prince of Wales paid me compliments," she said. "Princess Alexandra was very gracious, and I lost count of the distinguished people to whom I was introduced."

She smiled as she went on:

"I came home with my head in a whirl, and all I could remember the next morning was that the Marquis of Oakenshaw had asked me to dine with him that very night,

40

and I could hardly believe I had not imagined it."

"You must have looked very lovely," Tarina said.

"I did," Betty replied, "and that brings me back to my gowns! Come along, Tarina, we must start work, or I will never be ready to leave the day after tomorrow."

She rang a little gold bell that stood on the tea-table, and when the door opened and a footman appeared she said:

"Tell Robinson to come immediately to my bedroom. Has James gone to the station for Miss Worthington's luggage?"

"Yes, M'Lady. He should be back soon."

"Let me know when he returns."

"Very good, M'Lady."

The footman shut the door and Betty said:

"All you need to get out of your luggage, dearest, are the little things that you want to keep. Anything else, if it looks like what you are wearing now, can be thrown away."

Tarina gave a cry.

"That sounds very extravagant."

"You will not think that when you see the clothes I have for you. But there is no need to unpack them all, you just want one in which to travel. And I have dozens and dozens of hats and bonnets for you to choose from."

She jumped up and put out her hand to Tarina.

"Come along! I feel this is a Play in which we are both going to take part. In the past you have always been a very competent producer!"

They were both laughing as they almost ran, hand-in-hand towards the bedroom.

. . . .

The Marquis was frowning because if there was one thing he really disliked, it was having his plans to which he had given a great deal of thought, being interfered with.

Last night at Marlborough House, Lord Rosebery had drawn him on one side and he wondered what he was about to hear.

"When are you leaving, Vivien?" he enquired.

"Tomorrow."

41

"Good!" the Foreign Secretary exclaimed. "I have one more favour to ask of you."

The Marquis groaned theatrically.

"Not another!"

"I am afraid so, and I am hoping it will not annoy you."

"I am already apprehensive."

"I informed the Prime Minister that you had agreed to go to Siam, and he is very grateful, but he asks, as you are travelling there in your yacht if you would do him a favour."

"Am I to be confronted with one favour or two?" the Marquis asked with a slight edge to his voice.

"Actually one," Lord Rosebery replied.

"I am listening."

"The Prime Minister has a relative who is going to India and he would be very grateful if you would be kind enough to convey her there in comfort."

The Marquis's lips tightened.

He had already chosen his party with great care, and he had no wish to have somebody who might not fit in foisted on him at the last moment.

It flashed through his mind that he could say every cabin was full and to squeeze somebody else in would be an impossibility, but the twinkle he saw in Lord Rosebery's eye made him ask:

"Who is this importunate traveller?"

There was no mistaking the somewhat knowing smile on the Foreign Secretary's lips as he replied:

"Someone who wishes to join her husband in Calcutta. Lady Millicent Carson!"

The Marquis could not help a short laugh.

He knew the Foreign Secretary had deliberately made him apprehensive and was well aware that Lady Millicent Carson had been in his thoughts for some time.

She had in fact been pursuing him relentlessly for nearly a year.

Owing however to her husband being sent on a Diplomatic Mission to Russia, she had accompanied him there, and they had therefore been swept apart from each other, and she had only just returned.

In his usual way, the Marquis had not missed her. But if he thought about it, he looked forward to seeing her again and renewing what had been only a flirtation with lips and eyes but with the promise of a deeper intimacy when the opportunity arose.

It was not surprising that Lady Millicent had been clever enough not to approach him directly when she learnt where he was going, but to have made her request through the Prime Minister and the Foreign Secretary.

It was a subtle move which he appreciated, and there was a somewhat mocking smile on his lips as he said:

"You are well aware, Archibald, that I could not refuse what I suspect is an order from the 'Powers that Be'!"

The Foreign Secretary laughed.

"If you are honest, Vivien, I am quite sure that you have no wish to refuse Millicent the hospitality of your yacht, although it may complicate matters until you reach Calcutta. But I have never known you at a loss, however many strings you may have to your bow!"

Because the Marquis disliked any reference to his success with the 'Fair Sex', he managed to look disdainful as he replied:

"I have not the slightest idea what you are talking about! At the same time, I am sure a cabin can be found for Lady Millicent aboard '*The Sea Siren*'."

"A very appropriate name?" the Foreign Secretary said dryly, "and thank you, Vivien, for the offer of your hospitality. I know the Prime Minister will be delighted."

"Offer!" the Marquis exclaimed, raising his eyebrows.

He did not elaborate further and only when he was at home and writing out instructions for his secretary to carry out in the morning did he wonder how much Lady Millicent would interfere with his pursuit of Lady Bradwell.

The two women were both exquisitely beautiful, each of them a Venus in her own way, while at the same time utterly different from each other.

Lady Millicent was tall and dark, with flashing eyes and a provocative manner combined with a sinuous body that could drive any man wild.

Lady Bradwell to the Marquis was very much as Tarina saw her: she typified the exquisite femininity that Fragonard had depicted in his romantic pictures, and at the same time, which he found intriguing in so young a woman, she had an expertise that was very French.

"I shall certainly not be bored on the voyage," he told himself, "at least not at first."

Actually, the addition of Lady Millicent to the guest-list made their numbers even.

As well as Lady Bradwell, he had asked two old friends whom he could always rely on to be charming and good-tempered and for whom he had a deep and very real affection.

Lady Loraine and her husband were not well off, and the Marquis who was fond of them both, knew how much it meant for them to enjoy his hospitality.

He therefore seldom gave a party either in the country or in London without their being included.

He knew that Elspeth Loraine would smooth over any difficulties that might arise, and would play the part of hostess to perfection.

Her husband was an excellent bridge-player, a witty and amusing *raconteur*, and as far as the Marquis was concerned, exactly the type of man friend he liked to have with him.

The same applied to Harry Prestwood, who was with him continually, and was more important in his life than any other man he knew.

Harry was always hard-up because his father, the 8th Baronet, had taken in his old age, after being crippled by a fall in the hunting-field, to gambling.

"By the time my father dies," Harry had said despairingly to the Marquis, "I will be fortunate if I am left with the proverbial shilling. So he might as well give it to me now, and be done with it!"

"Surely you can prevent him from gambling so wildly?" the Marquis asked.

"How?" Harry questioned unhappily. "Every moment of the day he resents he cannot ride or leave the armchair in which he is more or less carried from his bedroom every morning. When he is bored he settles down to back slow horses, invest in 'Get-rich-quick' companies and, in a few words, play 'ducks and drakes' with every penny we possess.''

"Have you spoken to your Solicitors?"

"They can do nothing about it. It is his money as long as he is alive. The house which is falling to pieces for lack of repairs is entailed, and so is the land. But everything else is his!''

Because the Marquis was so fond of Harry he got his own Solicitors to investigate the position quietly and without the Baronet being aware of it.

What they discovered was exactly as Harry had already said.

Sir Roger could spend everything he possessed without anybody being able to stop him from doing so, and was already in debt.

"He goes in for every damned Lottery of which he hears,'' Harry said despairingly, "and to my knowledge he has never won so much as a bottle of ale!''

"I am very sorry, Harry,'' the Marquis said sympathetically.

"I am damned sorry for myself!'' Harry replied. "If it were not for you, Vivien, I think I would give up and go to Australia or Canada as a lumberjack.''

"There may be something you can do when your father dies.''

"I doubt it,'' Harry said, "and I suppose I shall just have to let the house fall down. As it is now, it would take thousands to restore it.''

The Marquis was deeply sympathetic, at the same time well aware that his friend was very proud.

He had only once offered Harry money and he had refused it almost violently.

"If you think I am going to sponge on you like the rest of those other 'hangers on' who are always knocking on your front door,'' he said savagely, "You are much mistaken.''

His voice deepened as he went on:

"I like you, Vivien, as I always have, and we have been friends since we were at Eton together, but I will not be beholden to you, or an object of your charity. Let me make that clear, once and for all!''

The Marquis had not argued, but merely assured Harry that he enjoyed his company, and expected him to be in attendance more or less every day.

This meant that Harry did not have to worry where his next meal was coming from and he could ride the Marquis's superb horses.

Although he had a small pokey lodging in one of the streets off Piccadilly, he was more often staying with the Marquis in the country, accompanying him to his Hunting-Lodge in Leicestershire, or going with him to Scotland to fish or shoot grouse.

Because they were such close friends, a great number of people invited Harry at the same time as they invited the Marquis, almost as a matter of course.

It suited most hostesses to have two extremely good-looking bachelors at their parties, and it was only ambitious mothers with pretty daughters who were likely to inherit a fortune who steered them quickly away from Harry Prestwood.

The Marquis had not thought of inviting a woman to amuse Harry because at the moment he was heart-whole, and there was no one who particularly interested him.

He therefore thought now that Harry could take either Lady Millicent or Lady Bradwell off his hands until they reached Calcutta.

After that he could concentrate on Betty Bradwell and he was confidently certain what by that time her feelings would be.

"I suppose it will all work out for the best," he said to himself.

At the same time he still rather resented being pressurised into accepting another guest aboard *'The Sea Siren'*.

When he went up to bed he thought that despite the fact that he had no wish to leave England at this moment, a cruise towards the sunshine might give him that sense of adventure that the Foreign Secretary had mentioned.

"A new orchid, or a star," he repeated to himself.

Then he laughed because it was so very unlikely.

CHAPTER THREE

Travelling to Southampton, Tarina thought she was definitely living in a Play which she must have written herself.

When things had been very dull at home and she was
struggling after her mother's death with the housework,
with the help only of a rather stupid girl from the village, she
had told herself stories.

They were usually adventure-tales in which she travelled
to strange places all over the world.

Often at dinner-time she would ask her father about some
country she had been visiting in her mind.

Because the Vicar had travelled a great deal when he was
a young man and was also exceedingly well-read, he was
able to produce books on the subjects they were discussing
or the land about which Tarina was enquiring, and they
would study them together.

She therefore knew a great deal about the customs and
characteristics of far-off places.

Siam had been a land that always seemed to her to be
mysterious, exciting and perhaps more typically Oriental
than its neighbours.

But never in her wildest dreams had Tarina thought she
would have the opportunity to visit it.

Sitting in a comfortable Second Class carriage which had
been reserved for her as a lady's-maid by the Marquis's
secretary, she felt as if she was being carried off on a magic
carpet.

She only hoped that the Genie responsible for her trans-
portation, who was of course the Marquis, would not prove
too frightening.

The more she heard about him from Betty, the more she thought he seemed in many ways an unpleasant, spoiled and in her cousin's words 'stuck up' person, whom she was sure she would dislike on sight.

Betty of course, was so excited at having been asked to be one of the Marquis's party that she talked of little else.

"I even heard about him when I was in Paris," she told Tarina. "The French are very impressed by Englishmen who have good racing-stables, but even more by their lineage and their position in Society."

Tarina laughed.

"Mama always said the French were snobs."

"Of course they are!" Betty agreed. "With the result that I met only aristocrats when I was in France, although some of them were young and ardent."

"They did not ask you to marry them?" Tarina enquired.

"I had only one proposal of marriage," Betty replied, "for I am not a Catholic and the older Frenchmen were all married."

She laughed as she added:

"I was quite certain that if I had accepted my only offer from a beardless youth, his father, his mother and his grandparents would all have refused to allow the wedding to take place!"

"It sounds very formidable," Tarina said, "and anyway, I am sure you would be more happily married to an Englishman."

"I am sure I should," Betty agreed.

She had a little smile on her lips and Tarina was certain that she was thinking of the Marquis.

She therefore prayed that he was very much nicer than she thought he sounded from what she had heard about him.

When they reached Waterloo station she learned that a private coach had been attached to the train to accommodate the Marquis' guests.

As Tarina was escorted by one of the footmen to the seat in the adjacent coach which was reserved for her, she had a quick glance at two very beautiful ladies wrapped in sables and accompanied by several gentlemen with fur collars to their overcoats.

Because it was bitterly cold and there had been snow the day before, Tarina was very grateful for the fur-lined cloak that Betty had given her.

When she unpacked just enough of the trunks in her bedroom to find a black gown, she had been worried as to what she could wear over it.

She had therefore gone to Betty to say:

"Everything is so beautifully packed in tissue-paper in the trunk you have given me that I do not like to upset it by looking for a coat. Do you think it would be possible for you to ask your maid if she remembers where she put one?"

"You need not worry about that," Betty replied. "I have the very thing for you."

She had gone to the wardrobe in the next bedroom to her own and drawn out a travelling-cloak which was not only lined with black ermine but had a collar of the same fur which also edged the front of it.

It was very beautifully made and obviously very expensive.

"I cannot possibly accept that!" Tarina objected.

"Do not be so stupid!" Betty replied. "I shall never wear it again. I bought it last winter to go to France, and even the French thought it was smart! It will suit you beautifully."

Overcome at owning anything so expensive, Tarina put it on and knew that while black was the proper wear for a lady's-maid, it was at the same time a perfect frame for her white skin and red hair.

She was however sensible enough to know that the last thing she must do was attract attention to herself.

So she swept back her hair tightly into a large bun at the back of her head and chose the plainest of Betty's bonnets to wear for the journey.

Even so, she had the uncomfortable impression that she did not look like a lady's-maid, and only hoped that the fact that she was supposed to be French would be the answer to anyone who looked at her questioningly.

49

She had however said to Betty the night before:

"I have been thinking, dearest, that the wisest thing for me to do would be to say that I am half-French and half-English to anybody who is interested."

"Why?" Betty enquired.

"Because it is so easy to forget to have a broken accent," Tarina answered, "and if anybody asks me, which is unlikely, I can say that my father was French and my mother English, and that for years I have lived in this country."

"Of course, that is very sensible," Betty agreed. "You are clever, Tarina! I knew you would act yourself into the part."

"Touch wood!" Tarina pleaded.

"That is what I am doing for myself," Betty said. "If you are nervous of the part you have to play, I am much more nervous of mine."

"I do not know why you should be," Tarina answered. "No one in the party could be any more beautiful than you."

"It is not a question of my looks," Betty said, "but of being with people who have their own special jokes, their own likes and dislikes and, what is most important of all, their own memories."

She looked at Tarina as if to see if she was following her train of thought, and went on:

"I am the odd one out, the stranger in their midst, and quite frankly I feel like a 'new girl' at School."

Tarina laughed.

"Why do you not cancel the whole trip and stay in London where you are already a success, and accept all the invitations I see on your writing-desk?"

"I can answer that in four words," Betty replied.

"What are they?"

"The Marquis of Oakenshaw!"

. . . .

Thinking of it now as the train steamed through fields white with the recent fall of snow, Tarina had the uncomfortable feeling that Betty was going to be disappointed.

Perhaps because she had Celtish blood in her as well as Austrian, or perhaps because she had been so much alone,

Tarina had an instinct, or what her father called a perception, that made her often see beneath the surface.

"We do not use our perception enough," the Vicar had said. "People have become lazy with civilisation. In the past, man, like animals, could scent danger, and was seldom deceived by words when he could look into another man's soul."

"Is that what you do, Papa?"

"I try to, my darling," the Vicar had answered, "and sometimes I am appalled by what I see."

From all Betty had told her Tarina's instinct where the Marquis was concerned, warned her that he was not worth the trouble she was taking to please him.

"If he is not aware that Betty is a sweet, charming, unspoilt, kind person," Tarina thought loyally, "then the sooner she forgets him, the better!"

She went on in her mind:

"If he wants sophisticated, exotic women, then he should look elsewhere."

She did not know exactly what sophisticated, exotic women were like, but her very extensive reading had told her there were always Delilahs in the world, and Liliths who had enticed Adam in the Garden of Eden!

Added to which there were Sirens, witches, sorcerers and villainesses as she had found in the books that filled her father's Library to overflowing.

They had belonged to his father, and his father before him, and it had broken her heart when she had to sell them.

Because they were old, they were what the Buyer called "out of fashion".

He had offered her a very small sum for them, and for one moment she had played with the idea of keeping them.

Then she had known despairingly that she could not pay for the storage.

Even if the new Vicar or one of the farmers in the neighbourhood would let her put them in a barn which was not in use, the rats or mice would eat them, or the rain would come in from the roof, and after a little while they would not even be readable.

She minded losing her father's books more than anything else.

She had spent so many hours poring over them, feeling they opened windows into a world she had never seen and never known in real life, but which became hers because what she had read was stored in her memory.

"I wonder if the Marquis will have any books on his yacht?" she thought, and decided it was unlikely.

She was certain since he was an acknowledged sportsman, he would not be a reader.

The Marquis's servants had ordered a hamper of food to be placed in the carriage beside her, and when it was luncheontime she enjoyed every mouthful.

It seemed a long journey to Southampton, and she wondered what Betty was doing and knew she was excited in a very different way from hers, at going to Siam.

. . . .

As it happened, Betty was actually feeling a little piqued when she looked at Lady Millicent Carson and knew she was the sort of beautiful woman who made her feel shy.

She had assumed from what the Marquis had said, when he invited her and the way he had looked at her, that she was to be his sole interest on the voyage.

When therefore a few moments before the train left Lady Millicent swept into the carriage, Betty could only stare at her in astonishment.

She had seen her on the platform as Tarina had done, but instead of talking to the other guests she had walked away out of earshot with a tall, good-looking young man who was clearly not one of the yacht-party.

They seemed to have a great deal to say to each other, and when Lady Loraine suggested it was time to get into the carriage, Betty had been quite certain that Lady Millicent would not accompany them.

Then as the doors were being shut and the Guard was standing ready with a whistle in one hand and a red flag in the other, she had joined them looking so spectacular that it was almost as if she made an entrance on a stage.

The Marquis who had been sitting beside Betty rose to his feet, and Lady Millicent had exclaimed:

"Please find me a comfortable seat not over the wheels. I am feeling too exhausted at the moment to endure any movement of that sort."

The Marquis assisted her to a comfortable armchair in the carriage which was arranged like a miniature Drawing-Room and to Betty's chagrin sat down beside her.

"I am so delighted to be able to look after you on your journey to India," he said.

Betty now knew how far Lady Millicent was going with them, and she listened intently as she replied:

"I am very grateful to Your Lordship, and of course I have written to tell my husband how kind you have been."

Betty gave a little sigh of relief.

So Lady Millicent was married!

Because she was delighted to know this, she was smiling as the seat which the Marquis had vacated was taken by a handsome young man.

"My name is Harry Prestwood," he said, "and I am one of Vivien's oldest friends."

"He has spoken of you."

Betty thought that Harry Prestwood was very good-looking, and before they had travelled very far she found it easy to talk to him.

"Tell me about yourself," Harry suggested. "Vivien told me you have been living in France, which was that country's gain and our loss."

Betty dimpled at him.

"That is very kind of you," she said, "and I am so excited to be back in England, and even more excited to be on this wonderful 'Voyage of Discovery'."

Harry laughed.

"Who told you it was that?"

"It must be, when we are going to such a strange and outlandish country as Siam."

"That is what I feel," Harry said, "and it will be my first visit there as well as yours."

"I am so glad," Betty said, "I shall not feel so ignorant

53

when I ask a lot of questions, and I am sure there will be many fascinating things to see.''

She sounded so young and ingenuous as she spoke that Harry said:

"That is just the right attitude. I am sick of people who are bored with everything because they have done it all before, and that, unfortunately, is too often the attitude of our noble host."

"At least he should be able to tell us what we want to know," Betty replied.

"I think the answer to that is that you must ask the questions."

Harry's eyes twinkled as if he was amused, but the way in which he was looking at her told her that he admired her, and it made her feel more sure of herself and less nervous.

She was, as Tarina had thought before they left Grosvenor Square, looking exceedingly lovely in a travelling-gown which was the same colour as her eyes, and a cloak over it in darker blue trimmed and lined with sable.

There were sapphires in her small ears, and a large sapphire ring on her finger.

"You look like a piece of Dresden china!" Harry said unexpectedly.

Again he saw the dimples that appeared every time she smiled and added:

"I suppose you have been told that a dozen times before."

"Perhaps two dozen!"

He laughed.

"Now you are trying to make me say something really original."

"I am waiting to hear it!"

On the other side of the carriage Lady Millicent was looking at the Marquis out of the corners of her eyes which had a little upward slant to them.

"I am beginning to believe," she said, "it is fate that we should be travelling so unexpectedly away from England at this particular moment."

"Why do you say that?" he enquired.

"Because," she replied, "when I was told that Roderick was being sent to India, I thought despairingly that I should never see you again."

"And that worried you?"

"If there is one thing I really dislike," Lady Millicent replied, "it is being intrigued by the first two pages of a book, then not being able to read any more!"

"We have at least three weeks to find out what happens in the next chapter."

"Whether that is long enough of course, depends on you."

"I should have thought that it depended on us both," the Marquis said quietly.

She flashed him a provocative look and pouted her lips invitingly.

The Marquis thought as he had before that it would be difficult to imagine that any women could look so beautiful, so alluring, and with a siren-like attraction that was extremely intriguing.

And yet when he looked at Lady Bradwell, he thought her pink-and-white loveliness was as fresh as a flower!

Once again he was comparing himself to Paris with a lovely goddess on either side of him.

However by the time they had boarded *'The Sea Siren'* waiting for them at Southampton, he was well aware that even if he wished to, it would be very difficult to escape from Lady Millicent.

If he had not made up his mind, she had.

He knew that just as she had manoeuvred herself into being his guest, she was also manoeuvring him into the position of becoming her lover before they reached Calcutta.

He was not unwilling to play the part expected of him, he was only wondering what he should do about Betty Bradwell, who attracted him as much if not more than Lady Millicent.

Then he told himself that there was the rest of the voyage to Siam and the long journey home after Lady Millicent had gone, and Betty would keep.

. . . .

When having settled his guests into their cabins the Marquis was alone with Harry in his private sanctum which was next to his bedroom.

"I must say, Vivien," Harry said. "You have excelled yourself by having two of the most beautiful women I have ever seen as your guests."

"I am feeling rather pleased with myself," the Marquis agreed.

"They are both exquisite," Harry said, "but I feel that Lady Millicent is cast in the role of the villainess, and Lady Bradwell is definitely the heroine."

The Marquis laughed.

"I am looking to you, Harry, to keep one of them amused while I am otherwise occupied."

"I guessed that might be my fate," Harry replied, "but for once I am ready to oblige, Vivien, without the slightest reluctance to play the part you have allotted me."

"Thank you!" the Marquis said sarcastically. "I had no idea you had reservations about it."

"Not on this occasion," Harry replied, "but I have in the past had too many of your cast-offs crying on my shoulder not to feel that I am never the Bridegroom, and certainly never the Best Man!"

"Poor Harry! I promise the next time we go adventuring I will ask somebody just for you."

"Thank you for nothing!" Harry answered dryly. "I have tried that in the past, and I can assure you it is very frustrating to know that when you are present the frail sex invariably look on me as a rather poor second choice."

The Marquis laughed again. Then he said:

"Do not be tiresome, Harry! You know I rely on you, and I did not invite Lady Millicent. She was thrust upon me!"

"I know, I know!" Harry agreed. "But she is a hungry huntress, and once she has unsheathed her claws you may find it difficult to escape."

The Marquis did not reply. He merely looked cynical.

Harry knew that however persistent a woman might be, the Marquis had never been possessed by anybody, and he

56

would get himself out of any trap, however tight set its jaws might seem.

The Marquis rose from the chair in which he was sitting.

"Stop talking about women, Harry," he said, "and come and look at my yacht. You have not yet seen it all, and I suggest we have time before dinner to go up on the bridge and watch us moving out of harbour."

"That is something I shall enjoy," Harry agreed, "and may I say before you ask me, that I think *'The Sea Siren'* is absolutely magnificent! I can only congratulate you whole-heartedly on your newest acquisition."

If Harry was impressed by *'The Sea Siren'*, to Tarina it was a complete revelation.

She had never imagined that any yacht could be so large, so comfortable or so attractive.

She had often thought how much she would like to travel in a ship, though her father had made her laugh with his stories of the discomfort of those in which he had sailed as a young man.

From the moment Tarina stepped aboard *'The Sea Siren'* following in the wake of the Marquis's guests, with the servants who had come down in the train from London, she had thought that it really was like a perfectly appointed little house.

"The only difference," she told herself, "is that it moves on the sea, instead of remaining stationary on land."

'The Sea Siren' had only been delivered a month ago from the Ship-builders, and Betty had told her that the Marquis had chosen every detail himself and invented gadgets which no other yacht had ever possessed.

As Tarina drove from the station in a carriage with the Marquis's valet, he told her how his Master had planned and supervised every detail of the building and the decoration.

"His Lordship's a perfectionist," he said proudly. " 'E expects everythin' to be perfect, and woe betide any one as fails 'im."

"He has certainly set a high standard," Tarina smiled.

" 'E certainly 'as!" the valet agreed. "And you'll

understand wot I means when you sees any of 'is other possessions."

He gave her a knowing glance and added:

"From all I 'ears, that's betting on a certainty!"

"What do you mean by that?" Tarina asked curiously.

"Well, your Lady's a real good-looker," the Valet replied, "an' that's 'ow 'is Lordship likes 'em."

Tarina instinctively stiffened, feeling he was being impertinent.

Then she told herself that of course was the way that servants talked about their employers.

"By the way," the valet said, "me name's Hunt, and I were wonderin' seeing as 'ow you're a Frenchie 'ow I should address you."

"Why not *'M'mselle'*?"

"That makes it easier," Hunt answered. "I suppose it's because you're from Froggy land you don't look like any lady's-maid I've ever seen afore."

Because Tarina was anxious not to talk about herself she said quickly:

"I hope, Mr. Hunt, you will tell me who else is in the party. I saw two very beautiful ladies at Waterloo Station just before I was shown into my carriage."

Hunt, who wanted to show off his knowledge of his Master's affairs, reeled off the names.

"Most of 'em are old friends," he said, "except for Lady Millicent Carson, who 'is Lordship's not known for long, and of course your Lady."

There was a pause. Then he said with a laugh:

"I was surprised at Lady M. joining us at the last minute. I thinks 'is Lordship'd be concentrating on your mistress. It appeared to be 'cut and dried' until the day afore yesterday."

Tarina had been determined not to ask too many questions about the Marquis.

She had always been aware that servants talked and, as her mother had said, nothing could be hidden from them. Yet she felt it was distasteful to pry into something which did not concern her.

At the same time, from the way the valet was speaking, she knew that Lady Millicent was going to prove a menace as far as Betty was concerned.

"Who is Lady Millicent's father?" she asked.

"The Earl of Hull," the valet replied, "and her 'usband's Sir Roderick Carson, who's in th' Diplomatic Service."

Tarina's eyes widened.

"She is married?"

"Of course she's married," Hunt replied. " 'is Lordship never 'as nothin' to do with unmarried girls."

Tarina thought this very strange. Then she supposed that as he was so much older he would find young unmarried girls boring.

"I often thinks and 'opes," Hunt was saying, "that the Master'll never get married. 'E says 'e wants to remain a bachelor, but you should 'ear some of his relatives pleading with 'im, beggin' 'im to have an heir and settle down."

He gave a short laugh.

"Jus' like a melodrama on the stage, it is!"

"How do you know all this?" Tarina asked.

"Sometimes when they're short-'anded, I waits at table," Hunt replied, " 'specially when we're at the 'unting lodge or in Scotland."

He grinned before he added:

"The Gentry always behaves as if servants are deaf and dumb, but I keeps me ears cocked 'cause it amuses me."

"So you think your Master will never get married?"

" 'E'll get caught sooner or later," Hunt replied, "but it'll have to be someone wily! As I always says: ' 'Tis the early bird as catches th' worm!' "

He laughed again and Tarina felt her heart sink.

If the Marquis really did not wish to be married, then why had he invited Betty on such a long voyage?

"He will change his mind . . he must change his mind!" she told herself.

And yet she was very conscious that her instinct was telling her that Betty would be disappointed, and the Marquis would escape once again.

Nevertheless, when she learnt from Betty that the Marquis had said that her State-Room was the largest and most comfortable after his, she felt her hopes rise.

It was certainly very impressive with a bed draped with blue silk curtains which might have been chosen especially as a background for Betty's eyes and fair hair.

The carpet was a riot of pink roses and blue ribbons, and the built-in wardrobes made both Betty and Tarina exclaim with delight.

"How can a man have thought of anything so clever?" Tarina asked.

She began to unpack one of Betty's trunks which had been brought into the cabin, while two others were placed outside in the passage.

As she did so Betty threw herself down on the bed, leaning back against the pillows.

"Thank goodness I brought enough gowns to last the voyage!" she said. "I will wear the prettiest ones first while Lady Millicent is with us. I can see she is the Serpent in the Garden of Eden!"

It was what Tarina had thought herself, but she replied reassuringly:

"She need not worry you. After all, she is married and going to India to meet her husband."

"She is already trying to take the Marquis away from me!" Betty exclaimed.

Tarina turned to look at her wide-eyed.

"How can she, when she is already married?"

There was a little silence until Betty said lamely:

"She can . . flirt with him. Marriage does not stop a woman from doing that."

"Well, it should do!" Tarina snapped as she lifted another gown from the trunk and hung it up in the cupboard.

. . . .

When the Marquis came down from the bridge to change for dinner he heard laughter coming from the cabin next to his where he had deliberately placed Lady Bradwell.

It sounded very young, natural and unrestrained laughter.

When he listened to it for a moment he thought it was very different from the rather contrived laughter of Lady Millicent and most of the other sophisticated beauties with whom he spent his time.

He had a feeling that they practised laughing so that it would sound musical and of course seductive!

But what he was hearing now was the joyous sound of two young people who were laughing as if they could not help it.

For a moment he wondered who could be with Betty Bradwell, then realised it must be her lady's-maid.

He had felt it was rather a bore that she had insisted on bringing one with her.

Women servants he had found were always a nuisance on a long voyage. If they were old they were seasick and cantankerous, if young they upset the crew.

But because Betty had asked him so prettily if she might bring her maid, he had acquiesced, knowing that Elspeth Loraine's maid never accompanied her on a sea voyage because she was too old.

However having broken his rule once he had no intention of breaking it again, and when his secretary informed him that he had received a communication from Lady Millicent regarding her lady's-maid, he had replied quite firmly that there was no available cabin for a maid.

She could, he added, get to India quicker by a P. & O. Steamer, and could doubtless take most of Her Ladyship's luggage with her.

He was quite certain Lady Millicent would be annoyed.

At the same time he had no intention of putting himself out for her, and he knew that if she was tipped generously, Lady Bradwell's maid could look after Lady Millicent too, with the help of Hunt.

His valet was quite used to unpacking for any lady guest there might be abroad any yacht he owned, as were his specially chosen and experienced stewards.

Tarina however was upset and worried when Betty said to her:

61

"Oh, by the way, the Marquis has asked if you would mind doing anything you can for Lady Millicent. She has not brought a maid with her, which I thought between ourselves was a blessing, and I therefore agreed that you would help her."

"Is that wise?" Tarina asked nervously.

"What do you mean?" Betty enquired.

"Supposing I make mistakes? Supposing she suspects that I am not a genuine lady's-maid?"

"Why should she?" Betty enquired. "You are so clever and quick, Tarina, that you will soon guess what is wanted, and not make mistakes."

"I hope you are right."

She looked at the clock and said:

"I had better go and ask her now if there is anything she wants, and finish your unpacking later. I expect you will want to wear the silver gown tonight, or perhaps you would prefer the blue lace."

"I think the lace," Betty said. "I am sure Lady Millicent will somehow contrive to glitter sensuously like a snake."

Feeling nervous, Tarina left Betty's cabin and crossed the corridor to where on the other side she had learned Lady Millicent was sleeping.

She realised both of them were at one end of a corridor which ran down the centre of the yacht and led to the Master Suite which was of course, occupied by the Marquis.

This took up the entire stern of the yacht, and consisted, Tarina was to learn later, of a very large sleeping-cabin, a small private Sitting-Room, and a large bathroom where he could if he wished do gymnastics.

But for the moment she was only concerned with Lady Millicent who in answer to her knock said: "Come in!" sharply.

She opened the door and remembering what Betty had told her, she bobbed a little curtsy.

"May I help you, M'Lady?" she asked.

"I certainly need help," Lady Millicent replied brusquely, "considering I was not allowed to bring my own lady's-maid with me!"

She was sitting on a stool in front of a built-in dressing-table wearing an elaborate negligée of scarlet silk, trimmed profusely with lace and dozens of small velvet bows.

"What would Your Ladyship like me to do?" Tarina asked advancing a little further into the cabin.

She realised that while it was the twin of Betty's cabin, it was not so attractive.

The vast bed was not draped with silk curtains, but had a large picture of a ship behind it, and there were other pictures of ships on the interior walls that did not have portholes or built-in cupboards on them.

It was, in fact, Tarina thought, a very much more masculine room than Betty's, and she thought that was why the Marquis had given it to her.

"I suppose you can arrange hair?" Lady Millicent said in a tone of voice of one suspecting it was very unlikely.

"I will do my best, if Your Ladyship tells me exactly what you want," Tarina replied.

"For the moment all I want you to do is to tidy it where it has been crushed under my bonnet," Lady Millicent said. "Tomorrow we can start from scratch and see how well you can manage."

Tarina did not reply.

She tidied Lady Millicent's hair, which was arranged, she saw, in a fashionable manner which meant it was very full and fluffy in the front, and swept up at the sides and back to a small knot on the very top of her head.

She decided it would not be a difficult style to achieve, and although Lady Millicent did not commend her, she did not complain either.

When Tarina had fastened her into a gown of emerald green glittering with sequins she could not help knowing that she looked beautiful, sensational and unmistakably as Betty had said, like the serpent in the Garden of Eden.

There was a huge necklace of emeralds which Tarina clasped round Lady Millicent's throat.

Then walking rather carefully because the yacht was now moving out to sea, Lady Millicent, carrying her head high, and with a rustling of her silk petticoats went from her cabin

63

down the corridor which led to the companion-way and the deck above.

When Tarina went back to Betty's cabin she found her still there.

"You have been a long time," she said reproachfully.

"Her Ladyship was quite demanding. I shall have to be very firm and say that I must see to you first," Tarina said.

"I think she is terrifying," Betty remarked. "She makes me feel as if I am still in the School-Room."

"Nonsense!" Tarina said. "Put your chin up, dearest, and tell yourself you are a thousand times lovelier than she is, and unattached. How can she hurt you when she has a husband waiting for her in Calcutta?"

Betty gave a little laugh and kissed Tarina on the cheek.

"I love you, and I am so glad you are here with me," she said.

"If she does get the Marquis to flirt with her," Tarina said as if she was following her own thoughts, "You can get your own back by flirting with Mr. Prestwood. Hunt, the valet, tells me he is unmarried and one of the nicest gentlemen he has ever known."

"That is certainly a good reference!" Betty exclaimed, and they both laughed.

Almost as if she was following Tarina's advice, Betty, when she entered the Saloon, moved not towards the Marquis, who was sitting talking to Lady Millicent, but towards Harry Prestwood.

"I am delighted to see you," he said. "I was beginning to be afraid that you had already succumbed to the rolling main."

"It is not as bad as that!" Betty protested. "If I am late, it is because I have to share my maid with Lady Millicent."

She lowered her voice and he somehow knew that what she had to say was amusing.

Harry's eyes twinkled.

"I am sure that is even worse than having to share a husband!"

Betty was trying to think of a witty reply when she realised that the Marquis was bringing her a glass of champagne.

"I would be very remiss if I did not tell you that I have just realised that what was missing in my new ship was you!" he said.

"That was a very pretty speech," Betty said, "but I am sure you thought it out while you were having your bath!"

The Marquis laughed.

"I understand that Frenchwomen always know how to accept a compliment, and you have been living in France."

"I am still very English, and rather suspicious of Frenchmen," Betty replied.

He laughed again and Harry said:

"It did sound rather glib, Vivien, and not up to your usual high standard of politeness."

The Marquis put up his hands in mock dismay.

"If you are both going to attack me," he said, "I must go to seek consolation elsewhere."

He went back to Lady Millicent as he spoke, and Lady Loraine, who was sitting on the other side of Harry and had been listening, said:

"I am sure, Lady Bradwell, it will be very good for our host if you tease him occasionally. I often think that Vivien has begun to take himself too seriously."

"You are quite right," Harry agreed. "The trouble is not that he takes himself seriously, but that everybody else does!"

Lady Loraine replied, lowering her voice:

"I think, Harry, the real trouble is that Vivien is too often with older people, and we forget he is still a comparatively young man. He ought to be enjoying himself far more than he does, and it worries me when I hear that cynical note in his voice, and see that mocking smile on his lips."

"I agree with you," Harry said, "but Lady Bradwell is young enough to make us all want to laugh, sing, and of course dance."

"She looks like blue sky we are all hoping to see by the time we reach the Mediterranean," Lady Loraine said.

"Now you are making me shy," Betty protested, "and if I fail to make our host laugh, sing and dance too, you will just write me off as a failure."

"That is something I know you will never be!" Harry said in a deep voice.

As Betty looked up at him and saw the admiration in his eyes, she told herself that Harry Prestwood was a very nice man.

She was quite sure that, Lady Millicent or no Lady Millicent, she was going to enjoy the cruise.

CHAPTER FOUR

Tarina awoke to see one of her shoes sliding from one end of her cabin to the other, and realised they were into a rough sea.

Her first thought was whether she would be a good sailor, her second was of Betty.

She looked at her watch and realised that she had slept later than she intended, but she had been very tired when she went to bed.

Not only was it the tiredness of exhaustion, but also of excitement.

One of the stewards had brought her a delicious dinner on a tray. As she might have expected, the Marquis had a very good Chef aboard and she ate more than she had ever eaten at home.

Then, after she had left everything ready for Betty in her cabin when she came to bed, she had unpacked one of her own trunks which had been given to her in Belgrave Square.

From what she had already seen from the black gown she was wearing, she expected some lovely dresses, but what she had not anticipated was that Betty, when she had finished with mourning, had discarded everything else she had been wearing.

There were not only silk petticoats in every shade of mauve, but there were also nightgowns that were the colour of Parma violets, and white underclothes decorated with lace and slotted mauve ribbons.

It was fashionable at the moment as Tarina knew to have ribbons run through almost everything: pillow-cases, chemises and occasionally gowns.

But she had not expected it on the exquisite silk or thin lawn nightgowns that Betty had been wearing, and because even a tiny strip of ribbon signified mourning, she had been determined never to wear them again.

As she unpacked Tarina kept asking herself:

"How can I be so lucky? Thank You, thank You, God, for being so kind to me."

She felt almost as if her mother was smiling at her in her pleasure that she should now have all the things she herself had enjoyed as a girl before she married a penniless Parson for love.

She had never regretted it, but she had said sometimes a little wistfully that she would have liked her daughter to have everything she had enjoyed – not only clothes, but Balls and parties and horses to hunt, and of course to be presented to the Queen.

"I am quite happy as I am, Mama," Tarina had said shortly before her mother died.

But when she had been left alone with her grief-stricken father with nobody to laugh or talk with, she had missed her mother so agonisingly that at times it was a physical pain.

When she finally unpacked she put on a nightgown trimmed with lace that was made of very fine silk and ornamented round the neck and the hem with several rows of Valenciennes lace.

"I could almost wear it to a Ball," she told herself as she looked in the mirror.

Then she remembered that she was a lady's-maid, and thought if anybody saw her they would know she was not what she pretended to be.

But at the moment thankfully there was no one to see her, and no prying housemaids to be suspicious.

When she got into bed feeling like a Fairy Princess, she once again before she went to sleep, uttered what was more a paean than a prayer of gratitude to the God who had guided her to Betty.

"Now," she said, "I am no longer afraid and so very, very happy to be here."

Because it was so exciting it had been difficult to go to

sleep, and now as she dressed hurriedly she thought she must ask Hunt or one of the stewards to knock on her cabin-door another morning, so that she would not oversleep.

Her haste was, however, unnecessary, for when she went to Betty's cabin it was to find her half-asleep and determined to remain so.

"Go away, Tarina!" she said. "If you think I am going to get up, you are very much mistaken!"

"Do you feel sick, dearest?"

"No, but I might do if I move about," Betty replied. "I shall stay in bed, and I expect everybody else will too."

"I think I had better go and see if Lady Millicent wants anything."

"I hope she is a bad sailor!" Betty said rather unkindly.

Then as if she was afraid to laugh in case it made her sick she shut her eyes and turned away from the light coming from under the blue curtains which covered the port-holes.

Tarina went from the cabin closing the door quietly behind her.

She knocked on Lady Millicent's door and as there was no answer she went in.

There was no doubt that Her Ladyship was fast asleep, and Tarina looking across the cabin saw a suspicious-looking bottle on a table beside her bed.

She guessed it contained laudanum, or some sort of sleeping potion.

She had learned that Society Ladies often soothed themselves with such concoctions which her mother had always said were dangerous.

At one time Betty had had a Governess, with whom Tarina had shared her lessons, and who suffered from headaches.

Whenever she had one she used to take a spoonful of laudenum and lay down. Then the girls knew they would be free to enjoy themselves for several hours until Miss Gordon had slept it off.

Tarina shut Lady Millicent's door quietly and thought that as her services were not required she was free.

As she moved away a steward coming a little unsteadily down the passageway said:

" 'Mornin', *M'mselle!* Are you ready for yer breakfast? That's if you're havin' any!''

"I confess to feeling very hungry," Tarina replied.

The steward grinned.

"I'll bring it in a jiffy," he promised.

Tarina went to her cabin, made the bed and tidied it.

She had realised by this time that the Marquis had designed ten State Rooms aft in the yacht, but four of them were comparatively small like her own.

The one next door which was not occupied by a guest contained empty or unwanted trunks.

Tarina's cabin was very compact, neat and, she thought, very pretty.

The brass bedstead was single, unlike Betty's and Lady Millicent's, but very comfortable and, as with the other cabins, everything possible was fitted into the walls.

She had a wardrobe, a dressing-table, and a number of drawers, besides a washing-stand.

The cabin was painted pale green and when Tarina was in the bed she felt almost as if she was beneath the sea.

The steward brought her a breakfast of bacon, eggs and sausages and told her if she was still hungry there was lots more.

It was a much larger breakfast than she had ever been able to eat at home, for beside the main dish there was honey and marmalade, hot rolls and toast, as well as banana and a tangerine.

"When we gets to th' sun you'll be able t' have strawberries," the steward said as if he was promising a child a treat.

"In January?" Tarina queried.

"You wait an' see," he replied, "and in India you'll enjoy mangoes."

When he had left her Tarina gave a little sigh of sheer delight. Then because everything was so exciting she felt she could not sit still.

She wanted to see the sea outside with the waves splashing over the bow.

Her father had often described to her the storms he had

70

encountered in the Bay of Biscay, and although she hoped this one would not be dangerous, she felt that she must try to enjoy it simply because it was a new experience.

"Do you realise, Papa," she said aloud as if to her father, "I am living all the things we used to talk about? They are really happening to me! I only wish we were here together!"

She felt a little constriction of her heart because she knew that what she was missing so desperately now her father was dead was the way he stimulated her mind and her imagination.

Many people must have thought it extremely dull for a young girl to live in a quiet little village, and have few companions except for her father.

But once he had recovered from the shock of his wife's death, Tarina found that every moment she spent with him was a sheer delight.

He talked to her as if she was a contemporary of his own age, and as he was extremely intelligent he made everything they discussed seem exciting.

"If you were with me, Papa," she said now, "you would be able to tell me everything I want to know about Siam when we get there. But first there is the Mediterranean, the Suez Canal and the Red Sea."

Her father had actually been at the opening of the Suez Canal at Oxford.

He had gone there soon after taking his degree as what was known as a *bear-leader* or Tutor to a rich young man whose parents had thought it would be a good experience for him.

It had also been a great experience for her father. He had described to Tarina the opening ceremony by the Empress Eugenie, and the excitement when the ships with their flags flying moved in procession through the Canal itself.

"I must remember, I must remember everything you told me, Papa," Tarina told him, "but the first thing I must do is to look at the sea."

She took her heavy fur-lined cloak out of the wardrobe.

Knowing it would be impossible in the gale that was blowing outside to keep on a bonnet, she found a black chiffon scarf in her trunk which she draped over her head and tied round her long neck to frame her small face.

Then she buttoned her coat down the front, pulled up the collar and set off towards the companionway.

She thought as it was still early that it was unlikely there would be anybody about.

She suspected that like herself most of the Marquis's guests had had breakfast in their cabins, if they were capable of eating at all.

When she arrived yesterday, a quick glance had showed her the general plan of the yacht, and she found her way quite easily from the top of the companionway to the door that opened onto the deck.

It was difficult to get it open because of the violence of the wind, but somehow she managed it, then stepped on deck to be spellbound by what she saw.

The yacht was ploughing its way through a sea that was covered, as the children would say, with white horses, and although there was a strong wind, there was also a pale sun shining fitfully through the grey clouds.

It was so lovely and so majestic that Tarina stood looking at it for a long time before very cautiously she edged her way along the deck.

She kept close against the superstructure until she reached a point where she could see the waves breaking over the bow as the ship pitched and tossed.

She dared not go too near because the spray was washing the deck and draining away quickly.

She stood for a long time supporting her back, and at the same time feeling the wind whipping small curls of her hair from beneath the black chiffon veil.

It was exhilarating, and she felt as if it swept away not only her fear of being exposed, but also her fear for her future.

"I should have more faith than to be frightened," she told herself.

Then as the ship plunged into the trough of a gigantic wave she staggered a little and had to force herself back against the wall behind her.

As she did so a voice startled her by asking:

"What are you doing here? Surely you know it is dangerous?"

As she turned her head she found herself looking at a man who she knew instantly was the Marquis.

He was in fact, exactly as she had pictured him, only even more handsome and more impressive.

There were cynical lines from his nose to his lips which Betty's description of him had led her to anticipate, and deep grey eyes which she thought were hard like the sharp point of a knife.

For a moment, because she was surprised to see him and because in a way he himself was surprising, she could not answer.

"Who are you?" he explained. "I thought you were Lady Bradwell."

It was then Tarina called herself to attention, and realising it was impossible to curtsy as she should she said:

"Excuse me, My Lord. I thought nobody would mind if I came out here to see the sea."

"You are Lady Bradwell's lady's-maid," the Marquis said as if he was thinking it out for himself.

"Yes, My Lord."

Tarina had no idea that with her red hair curling round her forehead and her dazzling white skin against the darkness of her cloak and veil, she looked anything but what she purported to be.

"You are obviously a good sailor," the Marquis said, as if he was telling himself why she was there.

"I hope so, My Lord. This is the first time I have been to sea."

He smiled and it swept the cynical expression from his face.

"The first time!" he said. "Well, what do you think of it?"

Without considering Tarina said the first thing that came into her mind.

"I am listening," she replied, "to *the music in its roar*."

As she spoke she looked away from the Marquis towards

the waves breaking over the bow and did not see the surprise on his face.

"You *'love not man the less, but Nature more'*," he finished. "Is that what you are feeling?"

"Of course I am," Tarina replied, "and I want

'To mingle with the Universe and feel
What I can ne'er express, yet cannot all conceal.' "

She spoke naturally as she would have to her father as they always capped each other's quotations.

She was still totally unaware that the Marquis was staring at her as if he thought what he was hearing could not be true.

Then as he was silent, she turned her face to look at him once again. Her eyes were very large and seemed for the moment to reflect the green of the waves.

"I see you know your Byron," he said. "At the same time, as it appears to be getting rougher than it was first thing, I suggest you go below, and do so very carefully."

"Of course, My Lord," Tarina agreed.

To go back the way she had come she had to pass him and he moved aside so that she could do so.

A wave crashing over the deck made him stagger for a moment and instinctively Tarina put out her hand as if to save him.

But it was unnecessary and as he reached over her head to steady himself she moved as quickly as she dared back towards the door.

The Marquis moved to follow her, and when she was inside he said in a dry tone:

"While I realise you are feeling adventurous, it would be very inconvenient if you were swept overboard where there would not be the slightest chance of saving your life."

"As I am particularly looking forward to visiting Siam, I promise Your Lordship I will be very careful," Tarina answered.

Holding onto the bannister of the companionway, she managed to bob him a little curtsy before she said:

"Thank you for being so considerate of my life. It is at the moment very precious to me."

74

She turned as she spoke and started to descend the stairs very carefully, so once again did not see the look of astonishment that crossed the Marquis's face.

Only when she had reached her own cabin and had taken off her cloak which was wet with spray did she think that perhaps it was a somewhat strange conversation to have had with a stranger – let alone the Marquis.

"Perhaps I should have said nothing," she worried.

But she knew that because she had been taken by surprise at his appearance, she had not considered at all what she said, but had just said the first thing that came into her mind.

She realised now she had not been in awe of him as she had expected to be and she wondered why Betty should be so frightened.

Then she thought that as far as she was concerned, she was not involved, not at all on equal terms with the Marquis. In his eyes she was only a servant who could be ordered to go below in a way he would not have ordered his guests to do so.

"I will have to find somewhere on deck where I can sit and not be seen," Tarina decided. "I can hardly stay below for the next two months."

Then she forgot the Marquis in thinking of the majesty of the sea and the way in which he had so quickly recognised her quotation from *'Childe Harold'*.

"I suppose he is well read," she told herself, and once again wondered if there were any books on board.

She was finishing her unpacking and very thrilled and delighted with every gown which Betty had given her, although she felt they were almost too good to wear, when there was a knock on the door.

When she asked whoever it was to come in, Hunt appeared.

"Good-mornin', *M'mselle*," he said cheerily. "I 'ears as 'ow you've been out on deck, an' getting into trouble for it as well!"

"Who told you that?" Tarina asked.

"The Master thought you was risking your life, and if you falls in the briny, he's no wish to turn th' ship round in this sea to go looking for you."

"Is that what he would have to do if somebody fell overboard?'' Tarina asked curiously.

"If you asks me, he'd just let the fishes eat you!" Hunt teased.

"I am sorry if it was wrong of me to go on deck," Tarina said after a moment, "but neither of the ladies wanted me, and I found the sea very majestic."

"You appreciates it more than anybody else does."

"Are they all sea-sick?"

"Not the Master or Mr. Prestwood, but Lord Loraine says he's not riskin' a broken leg, so he's staying in his cabin, and 'er Ladyship has told me to find 'er some books to read."

Tarina's eyes lit up.

"Books?" she exclaimed. "Are there books on the yacht?"

"Hundreds of 'em!" Hunt answered. "The Master 'as a private cabin filled with nothin' else."

Tarina clasped her hands together.

"Oh, please, if you are getting some for Lady Loraine, could you also get some for me? I have been longing for something to read."

"I'll find you books," Hunt promised. "What'd you like? A nice lurid murder, or love an' kisses? 'Is Lordship don't have so many of 'em."

"What I would really like," Tarina said, "is books about where we are going. Has His Lordship anything about Siam?"

"I'm sure 'e has," Hunt replied.

"We shall pass Italy, Africa, the Greek Islands, Egypt, and India before we get there," Tarina said.

"Half-a-mo!" Hunt exclaimed. "I can't take all that in but I've an idea of what you wants."

"Then please find me something about any of those countries," Tarina pleaded.

"What language do you want 'em in?"

It took Tarina a moment to remember that she was supposed to be French, before she answered:

"It does not matter. It is just as easy for me to read English as French, but I am not much use in Arabic or Siamese!"

Hunt laughed.

"I expects you'll make yourself understood, as I do wherever I goes with 'is Lordship. And if th' person I'm talkin' to's pretty, love's a language all women understand."

Because she thought that sounded a little familiar, Tarina looked away from him, and said in what she hoped was a dignified manner:

"I should be very grateful, Mr. Hunt, for any books you can borrow for me, and of course I will be very, very careful with them."

"You'd better be," Hunt replied, "or 'is Lordship'll have my 'ead! 'E don't expect most of 'is guests to be keen on reading."

It flashed through Tarina's mind that after the conversation she had just had with the Marquis he might not be surprised in her case, but in case he refused to lend her his books, she said quickly:

"Please, Mr. Hunt, do not tell His Lordship. But I do not think I could bear to go for weeks with nothing to read."

"Don't worry your 'ead, *M'mselle*," Hunt answered, "you shall have your books an' if 'is Lordship thinks they're for 'er Ladyship, I won't be telling 'im no lies."

He grinned at her and shut the cabin-door, and she heard him going down the passage-way.

'He is a nice little man,' Tarina thought.

She wondered if her mother would think it very reprehensible for her to let a servant talk to her so familiarly, or for her to intrigue with him to borrow the Marquis's books without his being aware of it.

Then she told herself her father would understand and waited impatiently for Hunt's return.

. . . .

The rough sea continued for three days and only on the fourth did Tarina awake to find the ship moving on an even keel with the sea no longer beating against the port-holes of her cabin.

Betty had refused determinedly to move from her bed, and Lady Millicent had lain most of the time in a drugged sleep.

There had therefore been very little for Tarina to do

except sit and talk to Betty when she wanted her or read.

Hunt became quite used to her asking him to change a book, only a few hours after he had brought it to her.

As he had no idea what she wanted, or what was available, he chose books from the private cabin at random when his Master was on the bridge or having a meal in the Saloon.

Tarina therefore found herself reading a mixture of French novels, Guide-books and studies of Oriental religions.

It did not really surprise her after her conversation with the Marquis to find he also had many volumes of poetry.

Somehow this seemed very much at variance with the idea she had formed of his character from what Betty had told her.

Then she thought that he might easily have filled his Library with the purpose of amusing his guests rather than himself.

At the same time, she found the books on Oriental religions fascinating and very instructive, and she wished her father had been there so that she could discuss with him what she had read.

He had often said that, while he was a Christian, he thought that Buddhism was a most just religion, and after she had struggled through several very erudite treatises on Buddhism, she had a hundred questions in her mind to which she wanted answers.

Hunt had found her a place on deck where he said no one in the Marquis's party was likely to notice her.

He explained that when the Marquis's guests did emerge from their cabins they would seat themselves towards the stern where as soon as they were in the sunshine and the heat, an awning would be erected.

It delighted Tarina that there was somewhere where she could read and at the same time breathe the fresh air because as a country girl she hated being cooped up.

As soon as the sea grew calmer Betty wanted to talk.

"Tell me what is happening," she asked.

"Very little, as far as I can make out," Tarina answered. "Hunt tells me that the Marquis and Mr. Prestwood spend a lot of time on the bridge, and they have luncheon and dinner together while everybody else stays in their cabins.''

"If I had any sense,'' Betty said, "I would get up and be with the Marquis. But when I do try standing up I feel dizzy and although I have not been sea-sick, it has been touch and go.''

"Then stay where you are,'' Tarina advised. "There is nothing more unbecoming than a green face and a heaving stomach!''

They both laughed.

"Anyway,'' Betty said, "Lady Millicent has not been able to steal a march on me!''

"I never believed anybody could be so quiet,'' Tarina said, "but when she is awake she is very disagreeable. It is 'fetch this!', 'fetch that!' Then she takes another spoonful of what Mama would definitely say was the 'Devil's Brew', and goes back to sleep.''

"Does she look very beautiful?'' Betty asked wistfully.

Tarina giggled.

"She puts grease on her face, and her hair is all pinned to her head to keep it in place.''

"It is a pity the Marquis cannot see her!'' Betty exclaimed.

By the time they reached Gibraltar the sun was shining and the sea was very much smoother.

It was however quite chilly, and when Betty got up and said she would have luncheon in the Saloon Tarina persuaded her to wear a warm woollen gown which was very becoming, and to carry with her in case she went on deck, a long fur coat of chinchilla.

She looked so lovely with her hair well arranged by Tarina that it seemed a pity to cover it, except that her bonnet with its pale blue ribbons was so becoming that she appeared to be made of Dresden china.

"You are beautiful, dearest!'' Tarina said when she was ready. "I do not believe any man would look at a Siren like Lady Millicent when you are there.''

"I hope not,'' Betty said. "And let us hope too that 'absence has made the Marquis's heart grow fonder'!''

"I am sure it has," Tarina said encouragingly.

She watched Betty move slowly down the passage-way and went back into the cabin to tidy it.

Two stewards arrived a few minutes later to make the bed, and she therefore went to her own cabin while they were doing so.

She had only just reached it when Hunt put his head round the door.

"Her Ladyship wants you," he said, and disappeared again.

Tarina went to Lady Millicent's cabin.

"I am told Lady Bradwell is up," she said sharply as Tarina entered.

"Yes, M'Lady."

"I will do the same, and now we will see if you can manage my hair without making a mess of it."

There was no doubt that by the time Tarina had finished getting Lady Millicent dressed she looked exquisite, but there was no improvement in her temper.

She was sharp and found fault with everything, while at the same time looking, Tarina had to admit, extremely glamorous.

When she was dressed in a green gown which had a coat to match it trimmed with ermine, Tarina thought that whatever her character might be like, her face was beautiful and her figure superb.

She did not however thank Tarina for what she had done, but merely gave her several orders, then swept away rather like a tidal wave, and just as formidable.

As she watched Lady Millicent go, Tarina gave a little sigh.

She somehow felt that Betty would never stand up to the competition which lay ahead, and that Lady Millicent would get her own way whoever tried to stop her.

As soon as she realised luncheon was being served in the Saloon, Tarina picked up the three books which Hunt had brought her early the day before and which she had now finished, thinking that here was her opportunity to choose some others for herself.

She walked along the passageway, opened the door of the Master Suite, and as she expected found Hunt in his Master's bedroom.

"Is it all right, Mr. Hunt, if I return these books you brought me, and choose some others?" she asked.

"Have you read 'em already?" Hunt asked. "I don't believe it!"

"I have read every word of them," Tarina said. "I am a very quick reader."

"Either that or a bit of a liar."

Tarina did not laugh, and as if he realised she was waiting, he said:

"Go on, then. Here's your chance to pick and choose an' you can tell me 'nother time what you wants me to bring you."

Without waiting to bandy any more words, Tarina opened the door which led into the Marquis's private room.

As she entered it she gave a little gasp.

She had not really believed Hunt when he had said there were hundreds of books there!

Now she thought how clever the Marquis had been when he had planned the yacht, in leaving three sides of his special sanctum for a large collection of books.

There were books literally from floor to ceiling and to Tarina it was as exciting as being let loose in an Aladdin's cave.

She hardly noticed the flat-topped desk, or the attractive furniture covered with red leather.

All she had eyes for were books and more books, and even at a glance she realised they were exactly what she wanted to read.

They were not old, or what the Book-buyer would have called 'old fashioned' and out-of-date like her father's books.

Instead they were all the very latest volumes written on every subject she could imagine.

As she looked along the shelves she felt as excited as a man who has just discovered a gold-mine, or struck oil when he least expected it.

Finally, as time was passing, she seized a large book of poetry, another on Egyptology, and a third called: *'Myths and Gods of India.'*

She saw there were several on Siam, and thought those could wait.

It was more important to take them in order, and the great joy was to know that there was plenty of time for her to read them all.

She carried them back to her cabin and thought with pleasure of the hours of reading that lay ahead of her.

Then she wondered if the Marquis had chosen the books himself, or if he had just given an order to his secretary to fill the shelves with the very latest volumes from a Bookshop.

Whatever the answer, she knew that if she had been happy before aboard *'The Sea Siren'* her happiness was now complete.

"I can read and read," she told herself with joy, "instead of like Betty and Lady Millicent having to fight over a man who more than likely does not want either of them!"

Once again her instinct told her that was the truth.

She did not know how she knew, she was only more certain than she had been before, having seen the Marquis, that he would not marry Betty, and, although he might flirt with Lady Millicent, she actually meant nothing to him.

"What is he looking for?" she wondered. "What does he expect from life that he does not already possess?"

Almost as if a voice spoke in her mind she knew the answer.

Then she quickly told herself if that was the truth she did not want to think about it.

· · · · · · ·

The Mediterranean, surprisingly hot for the time of the year, was not only as blue as the Madonna's robe, but calm as the proverbial duck-pond.

As they sailed eastwards Betty sitting under the awning which had just been erected over the aft deck realised that the Marquis was being completely monopolised by Lady Millicent.

82

She had been talking to him intimately all during lunch-eon, and now when he suggested they would all like to be outside in the air, she had somehow contrived to draw him aside and they had both disappeared.

Harry Prestwood hastily sat down beside Betty, and as if to divert her mind from what she was thinking, he said:

"You look lovelier every day, and I am tired of calling you Lady Bradwell, so can I be informal and say 'Betty'?"

"Of course," Betty smiled, "and I find it difficult to think of you as anything but Harry."

"That is what I want you to call me," he said. "Now let me start again by telling you how beautiful you are."

There was a note of sincerity in his voice which she thought made it different from the kind of compliment he had paid her when they first met and which had come so easily to the lips of the men she had met in France.

"I like hearing that," she said after a moment. "At the same time, I often think it is unfair."

"What is?" Harry enquired.

"That life is so much easier for a woman who is pretty."

"Not always."

She looked at him enquiringly, and he explained:

"Governesses, shop-girls, anyone who is in a subservient position, are pursued and very often ruined because they had an attractive face."

"I suppose that is true," Betty said. "But I would rather not think of it."

"Why should you?" he asked. "Everything around you should be as beautiful as you are. I would hate to see you worried or sad or frightened."

"I hope to be none of those things . . again."

"Were you happy when you were married?"

There was a little pause, then Betty said:

"I do not wish to talk about it."

"You have given me the answer I suspected."

"I am very happy now."

"Are you speaking generally, or of this particular moment?"

She laughed and replied:

"Both!"

There was silence for a moment, then Harry said:

"There is something about you that is different from the other women I meet night after night, at every party, every ball, every reception."

"I am glad I am different, but in what way?"

"I have been trying to explain that to myself," Harry said seriously, "and it has suddenly occurred to me that it is because you are a good woman, which is unusual in the Society in which I move."

Betty looked at him with a puzzled expression on her face.

"I hope I am good, but if I am, what do bad women do to make them seem different?"

"It is not exactly what they do," Harry said as if he was reasoning it out for himself, "but what they think. I have a feeling, Betty, that your thoughts are fine and beautiful ones and that you do not hate people violently, nor do you cheat, lie or deceive those who love you."

Betty gave a little cry of horror.

"I should hope not! But I cannot believe that most women are as horrid as you are making out."

Harry smiled.

Then he moved a little nearer to her as he said:

"Let us forget about other women and talk about you."

CHAPTER FIVE

Tarina, standing at the port-hole of her cabin, watched the party walk down the narrow jetty to which '*The Sea Siren*' was moored.

She thought first how lovely Betty was looking, and that Lady Loraine, with her sweet smile and soft, kind voice was someone of whom she would always be fond.

She had done for Lady Loraine only some small services but they had evoked not only gratitude but also praise and a sympathy that Tarina found rather touching.

"You are so pretty," Lady Loraine had said to her only yesterday, "that I am sure you could find something more interesting to do than being a lady's-maid."

"I am very happy as I am," Tarina replied.

"Then that is all that matters," Lady Loraine smiled, "and thank you once again *Mademoiselle*, for the excellent way in which you have mended my gown."

The two ladies walking carefully along the wooden jetty were followed first by Harry Prestwood, then by Lord Loraine, and finally by the Marquis.

Whenever she saw him Tarina could not help feeling that he was fundamentally different from anybody else, and although she told herself it was ridiculous he had a strange effect on her.

It was almost as if she vibrated towards him and she felt vibrations coming from him when she heard his voice outside her cabin or on deck. But she could not really explain it to herself.

She was vividly conscious of him all the time she was on the yacht.

Whether she actually saw him or not, she had the feeling that his personality was so strong that it was impossible to escape from him.

She had taken great care to avoid being on deck when he was likely to be taking exercise or with his friends.

She also slipped into his Study to borrow books only when he was at dinner or when they had put into some port and he had gone ashore.

It had been very hot in the Red Sea, and Betty and the other guests wanted to do nothing but lie under the awning.

"It is too hot even to talk," Betty told her, then added: "Lady Millicent seems to have plenty to say to the Marquis!"

Tarina did not reply, but as the days passed she had the feeling, although she did not say so, that Betty was not resenting Lady Millicent's monopoly of the Marquis as much as she might have expected.

Then something happened which shocked Tarina and made her feel that the Marquis really was as unpleasant as she had thought he would be.

It was a day when the heat had been almost stifling and without a breath of wind. When the party went to dinner in the Saloon, Tarina had felt she could not bear to be below.

She had therefore gone up on deck to her special place which Hunt had found for her.

It was well away from that part of the deck which was sheltered by the awning, so that there was no chance of her being seen by the Marquis's guests.

It was a lovely night. The stars filled the sky and were reflected in the smooth sea, unruffled except for where the ship steamed through it, leaving a glittering trail of phosphorus behind.

This was so beautiful that Tarina sat looking at it entranced.

Then she raised her face to the stars which seemed when she looked at them to hold a message for her, and for the whole worried and troubled world.

"Why do we have to make things ugly when there is so much beauty around us?" Tarina asked and sat spellbound by what she saw.

There was a pale moon moving slowly up the sky and its light added to that of the stars made everything seem as magical as the phosphorus on the water.

Deep in her thoughts, she was thinking of what she had learnt from the books she had read on the voyage.

She felt as if her whole mind and spirit responded to something that was just out of reach, and yet was part of herself.

It suddenly occurred to her that it must be very late because there was no sound of voices and she supposed everybody had gone to bed.

Feeling a little stiff from sitting for so long, she rose to walk back along what she thought would be the empty deck.

She had only just moved from her hiding-place when she was aware that two people were emerging from where the awning ended just ahead of her.

Hastily she shrank back into the deep shadow of the superstructure and leaning against it felt sure she could not be seen.

Then she realised that the Marquis and Lady Millicent were standing against the railing and she heard him say in a voice which seemed to her always to have a strange vibration about it:

"That is the star I want to show you."

He pointed as he spoke, up to the sky overhead, but Lady Millicent replied softly:

"I am not interested in stars, Vivien, but in you!"

She put up her arms as she spoke and drew his head down to hers.

She was wearing a glittering gown of sequins and tulle which Tarina had helped her into before dinner, and in the light from the stars and the moon overhead she seemed to glisten as if she had just emerged from the sea.

Tarina had never seen a man and a woman kiss each other passionately.

As the Marquis and Lady Millicent were locked together she had a strange feeling in her breast that was different from anything she had ever felt before.

The Marquis raised his head and Lady Millicent said:

"You excite me, Vivien, as you always do. I want to be very much closer to you than I am at this moment. Do not be too long, my wonderful lover."

The way she spoke, rather than the words she said, seemed to be vibrant with passion.

Then she turned and moved away with a sinuous grace that made Tarina think she was like a serpent sliding into the darkness.

The Marquis stood where he was for a moment, before once again his face was raised to the stars.

Then as he turned round the ship must have changed course for the moonlight suddenly shone directly into the shadows where Tarina was standing.

It lit her face and the Marquis could see her eyes very large and surprised looking at him across the deck.

For a moment he seemed to be turned to stone, and Tarina felt as if her voice had died in her throat.

Then in a strange voice he said quietly:

"I imagine you came on deck to look at the stars. Raise your eyes to them, and do not look down."

It was an order, and yet she had the feeling it was also a plea, although why, and for what, she had no idea.

She did not answer and after a second he turned and disappeared under the awning as Lady Millicent had.

Only when Tarina got back to her own cabin did she realise she was trembling, and she was also shocked and horrified.

She knew how stupid she had been, how ignorant and foolish not to have realised before that Lady Millicent was not simply flirting with the Marquis, but that he was her lover.

"How could she . . behave in such a . . way when she . . has a . . husband?" Tarina asked.

It was so surprising and so different from anything with which she had ever come in contact before in her quiet and simple life at the Vicarage that she felt her cheeks burning with embarrassment.

What had she seen? What had she heard?

"How can I have been so . . foolish as not to . . under-

stand that . . this is how ladies like Lady Millicent ...
behave?'' she asked.

Almost as if the knowledge swept over her like the waves
of the sea, she understood many things that had puzzled her
in the past.

She remembered criticisms she had heard of the Prince of
Wales, her father's disapproval of the ladies who were
always associated with him, and some of the things Betty
had said.

When Betty realised how ignorant her little cousin was,
she had quickly changed the subject, but Tarina now
recalled the expression in her eyes.

Lovers!

She had always associated the word with Romeo and
Juliet, or the love poems that she had read and to which she
had responded without, she thought, really understanding
their meaning.

That a married woman like Lady Millicent, who was travelling to India to join her husband, should go to bed with
another man seemed to her horrifying.

It was so scandalous that she could only lie awake in the
darkness thinking that Betty should not associate with anybody so fast and so immoral.

Then, almost like the serpentine movements of Lady
Millicent herself, came the question as to whether Betty was
prepared to play the same part in the Marquis's life.

''How could she do such a thing?'' Tarina asked.

Then with a sense of inexpressible relief she remembered
that Betty was free.

The Marquis could marry Betty, and as that was something she wanted perhaps she would be prepared to forgive
his present behaviour once Lady Millicent had left them.

At the same time, Tarina felt it was all rather horrible and
degrading.

Afraid she might hear the Marquis going to Lady Millicent's cabin or her into his, she covered her ears with her
hands.

'It is wrong, it is wicked, and Papa would be very, very
shocked!' she whispered.

But that was what she too felt deeply and for the rest of the night she lay sleepless.

· · · · · · · ·

When they reached Calcutta some days later, Tarina was inexpressibly glad to know that Lady Millicent was leaving them.

She did not say anything to Betty, and because her cousin did not seem as glad as she expected she would have been, she thought it best not to discuss it.

In fact Betty was so quiet after the yacht, having deposited Lady Millicent ashore, steamed on again, that Tarina felt she could not be well.

"Why do you not stay in bed today?" she asked since Betty seemed so pale and quiet when she called her.

"No, no," Betty said quickly. "Of course I must get up."

"You look tired, Dearest."

"It is the heat," Betty said petulantly, "but they say it will be cooler tomorrow."

It certainly was a little cooler with a wind blowing from the South-West but still Betty did not seem her sparkling, laughing self.

Tarina thought that she must be suffering because of the Marquis's infidelity.

"I am sure it will be all right," she told herself consolingly, "now that horrible Lady Millicent has left."

It was then that Lady Loraine asked her if she would be very kind and mend a gown that she had torn.

"I did not like to ask you before, *Mademoiselle*," Lady Loraine said in her soft voice, "as you had Lady Millicent also to look after. But if you could mend it for me I should be very grateful. I admit to being helpless with a needle."

"Of course I will mend it, My Lady," Tarina replied, "and now I have plenty of time to do so."

"I have always heard that Lady Millicent is very demanding," Lady Loraine said with a smile.

"Very!" Tarina agreed.

Her tone of voice echoed her shocked disapproval of the

dark-eyed Beauty and her memory of how disagreeable she had been.

"And now we can be a nice, cosy party," Lady Loraine remarked, as if she was speaking to herself. "Lady Millicent has always been nothing but a disturbing influence."

The way she spoke made Tarina long to tell her how much she disliked and disapproved of Lady Millicent, but she knew it was something no lady's-maid would do.

Taking Lady Loraine's gown which she was to mend she went to her own cabin.

There was only Hunt to tell how excited she was when they reached the Chao P'Raya River.

She had learnt from books in the Marquis's Library how important it was to the Kingdom of Siam, and that it had become known to western geographers as the *'Menam'* which meant *'Mother of Water'*.

It was because they controlled the river that the Ayudhya Kings were able to rule over nearly all of what was now modern Siam.

As they steamed slowly up the river towards Bangkok Tarina was fascinated by the number of boats, ships and barges of every description that were moving up and down the waterway.

She could understand the horror and apprehension that had been aroused the previous year when the French gunboats had opened fire on the Siamese coastal towns.

They had terrified the inhabitants in their wooden homes built on stilts that jutted out into the water.

When they anchored and Tarina could see in the distance the gilded pinnacles of the Temples and Palaces she felt that Bangkok was just as exciting as she had expected it to be.

The only thing that worried her was how she could get ashore and see everything.

However Hunt assured her that as the Marquis would undoubtedly be busy in conference with the King there would be plenty of time for her to see the City and everything in it.

"I only hope you are right," Tarina replied.

She went up on deck very early in the morning before

there was anybody else about, to see the river already alive with boats and barges, and the sun glittering dazzlingly on what she knew was the Royal Palace in the distance.

Now watching the Marquis going ashore wearing white trousers and a blue boating-jacket, she longed as she had never longed for anything before, to be with him.

Betty had told her that he and his guests had been invited to the Palace to meet King Chulalongkorn.

After luncheon they were to be shown round what Tarina knew would be one of the loveliest buildings in Bangkok.

"You are so lucky, so very lucky!" she murmured, then was ashamed of herself for feeling envious.

How could she be anything but grateful to have reached Siam, a country she had never imagined she would ever be fortunate enough to see.

She might not meet the King, but she could look at the glittering gold pagodas and the beauty of the river.

As soon as the Marquis and his party were out of sight she ran up on deck, and in the warm moist air she watched the passing boats and the people she could see on the shore.

Every book she had read told her that everybody in Siam smiled, and sure enough the children and everybody else did appear to be smiling.

Those in boats on the river waved as they passed, and Tarina waved back.

It was then that Hunt came to her to say:

"When I've finished all the things I've got to do for 'is Lordship, I'll take you ashore, *M'mselle*, if that's wot you wants."

"I would love it!" Tarina replied. "And there will be lots of questions I want to ask you."

"Ask away," Hunt replied, "an' I s'pose for starters you know that we're anchored opposite the Oriental Hotel, which is where all the 'nobs' stay."

He pointed to an imposing-looking building and added:

"If you looks through them trees just ahead you'll see Princes and Lords prancing around as well as millionaires!"

Tarina laughed and looked with interest at the Hotel half-hidden by coconut trees.

"It were built they says by two Sea Captains," Hunt explained, "for sea-farers and that's us, only we can't afford it."

"When did the Captain build it?" Tarina asked.

"Before you was born, about a hundred years ago!"

Tarina laughed.

"But you wants a chance to see the King," Hunt said, " 'E be a bit of a lad, seeing as 'e 'as seventy-seven children."

"I do not believe you!" Tarina exclaimed.

"Cross my 'eart," Hunt insisted, "and thirty-two of 'em sons."

When she thought it must be time for luncheon, Tarina went down to her cabin to find that her tray had already been put there.

On it was one of the Chef's delicious dishes, which being a cold one had not been spoiled by waiting.

It was too hot to eat very much and when she had finished, there was still no sign of Hunt who ate with the rest of the crew.

She therefore picked up the books she had finished reading and thought she would go to the Marquis's Study to change them.

The yacht was very quiet and she went through the outer door of the suite, then into his private cabin with the books which had made so much difference to her enjoyment of the journey.

They had, she thought, taught her so much that she felt in some ways she had become almost a different person since leaving England.

Then as she entered the Study she gave a little gasp for there propped up on two of the chairs with another lying on the desk, were three paintings.

As soon as she looked at them she knew what they were.

Quite a number of the books she had read on Siam had mentioned the mural paintings which adorned the walls of the Buddhist Temples and were called 'Jatakas'.

They illustrated tales of great antiquity, fables and legends which dated from pre-Buddhist days in India.

93

Tarina had read about them and felt she would never have the opportunity of seeing them because, as she knew, the best of them were not in Bangkok, but in Temples in the country outside.

And yet here were exquisite reproductions of them!

They were as delicately painted as a miniature might have been, but large enough to give a vivid representation of what they looked like on the walls of a Temple.

The murals, she knew, portrayed a world inhabited by mythical creatures and divinities, and their primary function had been to teach.

She looked at them, knowing that they portrayed courage, love, kindness, wisdom, forbearance, and truth.

There was a mystic quality about them to which she felt her heart, or rather her soul, respond.

She looked at one, then another, and tried to understand what they were teaching her as they had taught thousands of Buddhists all down the centuries.

The door opened behind her and thinking it was Hunt she slightly resented his interruption of her feeling of reverence which was almost one of prayer.

"Could anything be more lovely?" she asked.

"I thought you would appreciate them," a deep voice said.

Tarina gave a little exclamation and turned round to see that it was not Hunt who was there, but the Marquis.

She was still looking at him wide-eyed, feeling that his presence being so unexpected he swept everything away from her mind, and she could not even remember who she was supposed to be.

The sunshine coming through the port-hole made her hair gold with flashes of red that seemed to be duplicated in the paintings by which she stood.

Because it was so hot Tarina was not wearing the black gown that she felt was suitable for her position as a lady's-maid.

Instead she had put on one of very pale mauve that Betty had told her she would find useful in the heat.

It was exquisitely made, revealing the tininess of her

94

waist, outlining her hips, and flowing out over her feet in a froth of silk and chiffon.

Then as the Marquis's eyes seemed to flicker over her, Tarina managed to find her voice and stammered a little above a whisper:

"I . . I am . . sorry."

The Marquis shut the door behind him.

"I suppose you came here to change your books," he said, "as you habitually do when I am out."

"Y.you . . knew?"

"I could hardly believe that Lady Loraine could read so many books so quickly, and yet be so supremely ignorant about what they contained."

Tarina drew in her breath.

"I . . I am . . sorry . . it must seem very . . reprehensible but I was . . afraid that . . if I told your valet to . . ask your permission . . you might . . refuse."

She knew as she spoke that it was indeed exceedingly reprehensible for any servant to behave as she had done, and she said quickly:

"Please . . do not be annoyed with your man . . it was wrong of me to try to deceive you . . and it was only because your . . books meant so . . much to me."

"You have really enjoyed reading them?" the Marquis asked.

For the first time since he had come into the room, Tarina's eyes lit up.

"I was just . . thinking a little while ago that because of what I have . . read since I have been aboard Your Lordship's yacht . . I . . I have changed."

"Changed? In what ways?"

"I . . I know so much . . more than I did before . . and as my father would have said . . it has opened the windows to . . new horizons."

There was a silence until the Marquis said:

"And now you are delighted with my pictures!"

Tarina glanced at the paintings and said:

"They are . . wonderful! I have read about the *Jatakas* . . but I never thought I should ever be able to see one."

"And now that you have," the Marquis asked, "what do they make you think?"

Tarina was silent for a moment, then she said:

"I know their whole object all down the centuries has been to teach . . but I feel it is not possible to put into words exactly what that teaching . . entails."

The Marquis walked a little nearer to stand beside her looking down at *The Temiya Jataka*, a picture of exquisite colour, portraying dozens of different people in a variety of actions, all at the same time.

Each one was a miniature picture in itself, and yet they blended together as a whole, and as Tarina looked at it she knew the answer to the Marquis's question.

"I think," she said slowly, "these pictures are not meant to be looked at only with the eyes, but with one's instinct, or perhaps I should say with one's soul."

The Marquis was still. Then he said:

"You are putting into words what I have tried to express to myself."

"Then you do understand?" Tarina asked eagerly. "The important thing is what they give to each person who looks at them, and not what we *try* to learn from them."

There was a little silence. Then the Marquis said sharply:

"Who are you?"

As if he had shaken her awake from a trance, Tarina was startled.

Then as she hesitated for words he said:

"I do not mean your appearance on my yacht as a lady's-maid which I know, but your real identity."

He paused and added:

"I do not believe, for instance, that you are French, as I was informed you were."

Tarina felt she should protest and tell him what she and Betty had decided, that her father was French, while her mother was English.

Then because she had been brought up not to lie she felt the colour rise in her cheeks and knew as she blushed that she looked guilty.

"I am sure there is a reasonable and acceptable explanation," the Marquis went on, "for Lady Bradwell bringing you on my yacht, but I would still like to know how it is that you think in a very different way from any of my other guests, and that with regard to these pictures, you feel the same as I do."

"Is that really true?" Tarina asked. "I did not think . . ."

She stopped, realising that what she had been about to say was rude.

"That I could feel like that?" the Marquis asked. "I suppose it is understandable that you should think so. The fact is that when I was here four years ago, I found an artist copying the murals in one of the Temples up country and commissioned him to do some reproductions for me."

He smiled before he said:

"I had almost forgotten that I had ordered them, but the Siamese are very painstaking, and for them their time is unimportant. The artist brought these to me as soon as we anchored last night."

"I am glad, so very glad to have seen them."

"I know that," the Marquis said quietly. "But I am still waiting for an answer to my question."

"I think, My Lord, it is unnecessary . . and perhaps a . . mistake for you to . . notice me at all."

"That is a ridiculous answer!" the Marquis said sharply. "How could I not notice you? How could I not be aware of you, even when I do not see you?"

Tarina looked at him in astonishment. Then without thinking she said:

"H.how could you feel like that . . when I . . ."

She stopped, realising that what she had been about to say was too revealing, and the Marquis said quietly:

". . . when you feel the same about me!"

He looked down at his paintings once again and said:

"Do either of us really need an explanation? I have read every book on Buddhism that I have here on my shelves. Each one tells us quite clearly that this life is only one of many."

He paused and went on more slowly:

"If you and I are vitally aware of each other, it is because we have met before and our vibrations, or what you call our spirits, have a truer perception than that which our eyes give us."

"Do you . . really believe that?"

"I am sure of it," the Marquis answered, "and I think you are too."

She looked away from him and said:

"My father and I often discussed it. He thought that Buddhism was the only just and logical religion, and he thought when one delved into its philosophy that it fitted in perfectly well with traditional Christian doctrine."

The Marquis gave a short laugh.

"And now, having said all that, suppose you tell me who you are, unless of course you have stepped out of one of these murals in order to amuse and bewilder me."

"I think that is a very good . . explanation," Tarina answered, "so, please, My Lord, can we just . . leave it . . like that?"

She saw he was about to speak, and added quickly:

"But as I think it is unlikely that I can step back into the picture again, I should be grateful if Your Lordship would carry me home in the same manner in which I came here."

For the first time it struck her that if the Marquis was back, then the rest of the party must be back also and she said quickly:

"If Her Ladyship has returned I should go to her."

"There is no hurry," the Marquis assured her. "Lady Bradwell and the rest of my party are being shown around the Palace. I have seen it before, and therefore, having finished my business with the King, I came back to the yacht."

"Another time I . . must be more . . careful!" Tarina said. "I can only apologise again for . . reading Your Lordship's books without your permission."

The Marquis made a little gesture with his hand.

"My Study is yours, and I also hope you will enjoy my paintings."

Tarina drew in her breath.

"Thank you . . thank you!" she said. "But 'enjoy' is not quite the right word. I suppose really they enthrall me! At the same time, I feel that just to look at them will enlighten me more than a pile of books on the subject."

She spoke with a rapt little note in her voice which the Marquis did not miss. Then he said:

"I am still waiting to hear where you learnt so much about subjects which I can honestly say I have never before discussed with a woman."

Tarina thought she was safe to be frank, and she said:

"My father was a classical scholar, My Lord, and got his Doctorate at Oxford for a treatise he wrote on Oriental Philosophy."

"And having taught you so much, your father than allowed you to take this absurd position as a lady's-maid?"

"M.my father is . . dead!"

"So that is why you are wearing mauve!" the Marquis said. "And may I commend you on your very attractive and very expensive gown."

Now there was a note of suspicion in his voice that Tarina did not understand, and because there was something about the Marquis which made her drop her guard, she replied:

"Every time I put on one of the beautiful gowns I now possess I say a prayer of thankfulness at being able to own anything so lovely."

Even as she spoke she remembered that when she had seen the Marquis kissing Lady Millicent on deck and understood what was happening later, she had thought it ugly.

She had then felt not only horror and disgust that a married woman should behave in such a manner, but also from a slightly different way that the Marquis himself should do so.

He must have sensed what she was thinking because her eyes were very expressive, for he said sharply:

"I told you to look up at the stars and forget the way in which they are so often reflected in a distorted manner."

She did not pretend not to understand what he was saying, and after a moment she said:

"What is . . wrong and . . wicked . . spoils the beauty that . . God gave us."

99

"He also made us human," the Marquis said, "but because you are very young, you are intolerant of human weakness. When you are older you will understand that a man must seek happiness where he can find it."

Tarina made a helpless little gesture with her hands.

"You are right," she said in a low voice, "and I realise I am very . . ignorant . . and I expect very . . foolish."

"I would not call you either of those things," the Marquis said, "but try not to spoil yourself. One cannot touch pitch without being defiled."

Tarina looked at him in a startled manner and he said:

"Not only is it people's actions which spoil them, but their thoughts. What you are thinking now is alien to yourself, and not what my pictures are telling you."

"You are right . . of course you are . . right!" Tarina said in a low voice, "and it is . . something I should have . . known for . . myself."

"And you will therefore forget anything that has perturbed you?"

"I will . . try," she said humbly, "but sometimes it is . . difficult."

"It is always difficult," the Marquis said. "At the same time, if everything was easy, there would be nothing for which to fight, nothing to achieve."

Tarina gave a little cry.

"That is true, and when one has reached the horizon, there is always another one ahead. How can I have been so stupid as . . not to have . . remembered that?"

"Why did you forget it?"

"Because I was . . frightened."

As she spoke she thought how desperate she had been when her father died, and she found how little money she had.

She could remember praying frantically all the while she was going to London that Betty would help her.

Then when she least expected it, like the sudden shining of a rainbow in an overcast sky, she had been brought on this magical voyage and the darkness had gone, and everything was light.

"A voyage of discovery!" she said almost beneath her breath.

The Marquis started.

He remembered that was what the Foreign Secretary had said to him, and how he had finished by saying he might find the star he was always seeking.

As if what he was thinking perturbed him he walked across the room to reach up to the top shelf and take down several books.

"You have not yet read these," he said. "When you have done so, I shall be interested to hear what they mean to you, both to your mind and even more to your spirit."

Tarina took them from him, well aware that something had changed the course of their conversation abruptly and now he wished her to go.

Carrying the books she walked towards the door. Then she looked back to bob him a little curtsy and say:

"Thank you, My Lord . . thank you . . very much!"

She shut the door quietly behind her, then almost ran down the passage into her own cabin.

She had an inescapable feeling that she was running away from something overwhelming, and at the same time menacing, from which there would be no escape, now or ever.

Because she was aware that her heart was beating in a strange manner and she felt as though she had passed through a strange experience that was somehow mystic and at the same time bringing about a complete upheaval in her mind, she felt afraid.

How could she have talked to the Marquis, of all people, in such a manner?

How could she have felt so intimate as to express her real thoughts and feelings?

And how could he have asked her such questions, and at the same time telling her that he had been aware of her vibrations, just as she had been aware of his.

"I must be dreaming . . he could not have said . . that!" Tarina argued with herself.

Then as she sat down on her bed and tried to think, it

seemed to her that everything was jumbled in her mind to the point where like a jig-saw to which there was no starting point she could not begin to sort it out.

All she knew was that the Marquis was very different from what she had believed him to be, or what anyone else seemed to have found him.

If she had really heard what he said and not imagined it, then everything that she had listened to and which had made up a picture of a spoilt, cynical, dissolute man pursuing beautiful women was untrue.

While that picture portrayed perhaps half of the man the other half, which he had kept very secret, was entirely different.

It was as if she was seeing evil demons and the celestial devas of the murals united in one human being.

Now she could understand for the first time how her father had said that every man had God and the Devil within him, and the freedom to choose which should be his guide.

Then as she sat thinking of the Marquis, tinglingly conscious that something within herself reached out towards him, and that she had been vitally aware of him ever since she had come aboard *'The Sea Siren'*, she felt she was being disloyal to Betty.

It was Betty who had brought her here, and Betty, whom she loved and wanted to help, who wished to marry the Marquis.

"I am sure he will . . make her very . . happy," Tarina said aloud.

Then she almost winced at the pain that such an idea gave her, and knew incredibly and with dismay the reason for it.

CHAPTER SIX

Tarina found it impossible to sleep.

She lay awake thinking of the Marquis and of all the strange things that had happened to her since she had left London.

Then as the first glint of light came through the port-holes, she got out of bed to stand watching the sky gradually turn from sable to grey, and the stars beginning to fade.

She was thinking as she did so how the Marquis had told her to look at the stars when she heard a faint sound on the other side of the cabin and turned to look at the door.

To her astonishment she saw a piece of paper being pushed underneath it.

She picked it up and saw a strong upright hand-writing, which she knew without being told belonged to the Marquis.

"If you are awake, would you like to come with me to the Floating Market? Go to the jetty beside us which belongs to the Oriental Palace."

She read the words first in astonishment, then with a rising sense of excitement.

She had heard about the Floating Market and how it was unique to Bangkok, but because she knew it took place very early in the morning she had thought it would be one thing she would never have a chance of seeing.

Moved by the urgency not only of seeing the Marquis, but of not keeping him waiting, she hurriedly washed and dressed and without really thinking, put on the first gown she took out of her wardrobe.

Then as she glanced at herself in the mirror to tidy her hair she realised she was wearing a very pretty cotton dress that she was sure Betty had chosen for herself in Paris.

There was something very unusual about the way it was cut and the decoration of broderie anglaise which was run through with mauve ribbons.

It was so pretty and yet so simple that it had a special *chic* of its own.

She knew as she arranged her hair that there was a hat with not too large a brim to go with it.

That was of white muslin skilfully trimmed with mauve ribbons, and it was, Tarina thought, exactly what a young girl should wear.

She wondered if it was too young for her, and knew it was definitely far too smart for a lady's-maid.

Then she told herself there was no time to change and picking up her gloves she slipped out through her cabin-door into the dimness of the passage-way.

There appeared to be nobody about and everything was very quiet.

She hurried up on deck, to find there was no sign of any servants, but a door was open and she thought it must have been unbolted by the Marquis.

It took only a few minutes to walk down the jetty, and then at the end of it to step into the garden of the Oriental Palace.

She was aware that the jetty that belonged to the Hotel was at the other end of the garden, and she walked beneath the coconut trees on a path which led her to where, as she had expected, the Marquis was waiting for her.

As she walked towards him she saw his eyes flicker over her gown and her hat. She hoped that he was admiring her, but she was not sure.

Then as she reached him she said a little breathlessly:

"Thank you . . thank you! I wanted so . . much to see the Floating Market, and was . . afraid it was an . . impossibility."

"I think you will enjoy it," he said. "There is a boat waiting for us."

It was a rather strange boat, quite unlike one Tarina had ever seen before.

She and the Marquis sat in the front, there was a partition across the centre of the boat, and behind there were two oarsmen and another man to steer.

It made Tarina feel that she and the Marquis were entirely private, and she was quite certain anyway that nothing they said would be understood by those behind.

As they moved out immediately into the river the darkness was giving way to light, and Tarina knew that in a very few minutes the first rays of the sun would be coming up over the horizon.

There were only a few stars fading in the sky above them, and it was that exquisite, mystic moment between dark and light when even the world seems to hold its breath.

But the river itself was busy.

There were boats of every description moving out from where they had been moored all night, and already the ferries were filled with Siamese men going to work.

They moved for a little while in silence. Then the Marquis said:

"I found it difficult to sleep last night, and when I thought over our conversation together I still find it very surprising."

"Perhaps that is what your pictures . . . meant us . . to feel," Tarina replied.

"So that we should search for their real meaning?" the Marquis asked.

"That is what . . everybody who . . sees them should . . try to discover," Tarina replied.

There was silence. Then the Marquis asked:

"What is your name?"

"Tarina!"

"A strange name, but it suits you. I have never known anybody of that name before."

"It was the name of my great-grandmother, who was Austrian."

The Marquis smiled.

"That accounts for the colour of your hair, and I knew I was right in thinking you are not French."

Because Tarina did not wish to have to go into

explanations as to why she was called 'Janzé' she merely looked away from him towards the banks of the river which were gradually coming alive.

Women were coming out of the wooden houses that reached out on stilts over the water, to hang out their washing.

Children were waving to the boats passing by and several brown-bodied little boys were splashing about in the river, holding onto a small raft made of a few pieces of wood hammered together.

They were all smiling, and Tarina said:

"This is a happy land. Many of the people are very poor, as I can see, but they smile and laugh, and seem to find life entrancing, as it should be."

"And beautiful," the Marquis said quietly.

She knew that once again he was telling her that she should not think of anything ugly.

It took quite a long time to reach the entrance to the part of the river where the Floating Market took place.

There was so much of interest to look at that it seemed to Tarina only a few minutes before they entered a *klong* or a narrow tributary of the main river following in the wake of several boats which were all obviously seeking the same objective.

Then as the *klong* grew narrower and narrower, there were houses on each side with slatted verandahs all built on stilts with a little platform just above the water level and steps from it leading up to the house above.

But what was fantastic was the number of boats or *sampans* on the *klong* itself.

Each one, propelled by a man or a woman in a basket hat, by a long-handled oar, was filled to capacity with their wares, mostly fruits and vegetables.

The strawberries, the radishes and the water-melons made brilliant splashes of colour against the cucumbers, pineapples, beans and mushrooms of every description.

There were also *sampans* which were selling pots and pans, meat, fish, noodles, and even charcoal.

As the sun rose a moist heat seemed to come up like a tidal

wave to envelope everything and the boat-keepers put up large umbrellas to protect their wares.

Their boat proceeded through the midst of those buying and selling, and Tarina found it difficult to decide whether to look right or left for the most excitement and interest.

She had never before seen anything like the Floating Market.

Although everybody was busily engaged in selling their wares and obviously entering into long and complicated Oriental bargaining over the price, they were still smiling and good-tempered.

They rowed on and Tarina's excitement at what she was seeing was like that of a child at its first Pantomime.

It was all so thrilling that she was not aware as she pulled off her hat to see better, that the Marquis was watching her. Her red hair gleamed with the lights from the strange surroundings.

Only when after they had been there for a long time and the boat turned round did she give a little sigh and say:

"I never imagined anything could be so attractive, so pretty and so unusual."

"I thought you would enjoy it," he said.

On their return journey the chatter of voices, the sunshine and the kaleidoscope of colour seemed to intensify and be even more beautiful than it had been when they first arrived.

Only when they were once again back on the main river did Tarina say:

"How can I thank you for showing me something so unforgettable and so uniquely Siamese?"

As she finished speaking she raised her eyes to the Marquis, and there was an expression on his face she thought she had never seen before.

He looked at her for a long moment. Then he said:

"What are we going to do, Tarina, about us?"

For a moment she thought she must have misunderstood him.

Then as if he told her without words what he was thinking she looked away quickly.

"I . . I do not . . understand."

107

"I think you do," he answered, "and that is a question I have been asking myself all through the night."

"I think the answer . . if you must have one . . My Lord . . is . . nothing."

"Why should you say that?" he asked sharply.

She hesitated for a moment. Then she said in a low voice:

"You are . . well aware . . as I am . . that I should not be . . here with you now. It would cause . . a great deal of comment and . . surprise . . if Your Lordship's guests . . knew of it."

"There is no reason for them to know," the Marquis objected. "At the same time, I still want a reasonable answer to my original question."

Tarina did not reply, and after a moment he said:

"You are well aware that I cannot lose you. I want to talk to you, I want to know why you feel as I feel over the *Jatakas* and a great many other things. But it will be difficult for us to meet while we are both on the yacht."

Tarina did not speak but continued to look ahead, and the Marquis went on:

"I know what I want to suggest to you, but I am afraid to do so."

For a moment Tarina was puzzled.

Then an idea came to her which made her say without thinking.

"Y . you . . cannot mean . . you cannot . . think . . ."

Her words were incoherent. Then the Marquis said fiercely and in a tone he had not used to her before:

"Who gave you that gown?"

The question seemed to Tarina to have nothing to do with what they were talking about.

Then the harshness of his voice, and what a quick glance told her was the suspicion in his eyes, made her feel that she had stepped away from the beauty and sunshine of the Floating Market into the darkness of reality.

Involuntarily a picture formed in front of her eyes of the Marquis kissing Lady Millicent.

She could hear Lady Millicent's voice as she called him 'a wonderful lover' before she had moved away under the awning.

She stiffened, and the Marquis must have known by the expression on her face what she was thinking, because he said quickly:

"I do not wish to shock you. At the same time, I want an answer to my question as to who gave you that gown."

Because she felt bewildered both by his attitude and her own thoughts, Tarina said weakly:

"It . . it was a . . friend."

"That was what I surmised," the Marquis said.

The cynical note in his voice was very obvious and reading his thoughts Tarina said angrily:

"How can you . . think such . . things about . . me? How can you own . . anything as beautiful and as . . spiritual as the *Jatakas*, and at the same time . . imagine anything so ugly and so . . degrading?"

She was not certain exactly what it would have implied if a man had paid for her gowns, except that she was sure that in the Marquis's eyes it meant he had been her lover, as he had been the lover of Lady Millicent.

"If I am wrong, please forgive me," the Marquis said quickly.

Now he was speaking in a very different tone of voice.

"Of course you are . . wrong!" Tarina said, "and I consider the fact that you should think such . . things about me is . . insulting and . . humiliating!"

"Have you asked yourself how you are so sure that was what I was thinking?" the Marquis asked. "And how I know, Tarina, exactly what you are feeling now?"

She did not answer and after a moment he said:

"Once again I am saying – what can we do about us? How can it be possible for us to leave each other when there is so much more to discover?"

"We . . must not . . talk about it," Tarina said quickly.

"Then what am I to do?" the Marquis asked.

Tarina said the first thing that came into her mind.

"You asked Be . . Lady Bradwell to . . come as your guest on this cruise and she . . thought it was because you . . intended to ask her to . . marry you."

"To marry her?"

109

There was no doubt of the surprise in the Marquis's voice, and because he spoke a little louder than he had before, Tarina turned to look at him.

Then she gave a little cry of sheer horror.

"D.do you . . mean? Are you saying . . that you meant . . .?"

It was impossible for her to go any further!

It was as if once again her innocence and her ignorance of social life was thrust on one side by a rough hand.

She knew without more words that the Marquis had intended to make love to Betty and had only been put off by the intervention of Lady Millicent.

She told herself that Betty would never have consented to such a thing.

Then things she had said when they talked of the Marquis rose to confront her and she suddenly realised that Betty had never once said in actual words that she wished to marry the Marquis.

"No, no . . it cannot be true!" Tarina said beneath her breath. "It is . . wrong . . wicked . . and I would never . . allow her to do . . such a thing."

"I told you," the Marquis said quietly, "that I did not want to shock you."

"You *have* . . shocked me!" Tarina cried. "Although I know nothing of Society, except for what I have . . seen since I have been on . . your yacht. I am now aware of what is meant by 'self-respect', and that is something no one shall . . ever take from . . me!"

She felt herself tremble at the intensity of her feelings, and she found it difficult not to burst into tears.

It was almost as if the happiness and the innocence of childhood had been suddenly snatched away from her, and she suddenly found herself grown up.

To her she found herself in an alien and terrifying world which she did not understand.

As if once again he understood what she was feeling the Marquis reached out and took her hand in his.

"Forgive me," he said. "I had no wish to upset you. I was being selfish and thinking entirely of myself. But you are right. I did not realise how innocent you are."

"I am . . not any . . longer," Tarina said in a trembling tone.

"I told you to look up to the stars, and not at their reflection in the mud below.

"That is what I . . tried to do . . but now that I know the mud is . . there it has . . spoilt everything."

She felt his fingers tighten on hers as he said:

"I do not think you have studied my pictures very carefully. The Prince was always tempted by evil demons, and was only saved with the greatest difficulty at the very last moment by a holy Deva."

Tarina was silent.

She understood what he was saying to her, and while she thought it wrong that he should be holding her hand she somehow wanted to cling onto him.

With her new perception she was lost in a frightening world which she had been too blind and ignorant to be aware of until this moment.

She could see all too clearly Lady Millicent's dark, upturned eyes, her pouting, seductive lips, the sinuous manner in which she moved.

And she knew, as if the Marquis was telling her so, that she was one of the temptations that he had not been able to resist.

Yet she had left the yacht, and he had somehow survived.

"I think," the Marquis said interrupting her thoughts, "you are the 'Deva' who has been sent to help me, and guide me away from the temptations of the demons back onto the path of righteousness."

Because he was speaking with a sincerity she had somehow not expected, Tarina looked at him to be quite sure he was not teasing her.

"I have no . . power to . . interfere in your life in . . any way," she murmured. "It is yours, and only . . you can guide and . . direct it."

He shook his head.

"That is not true. For every man there is a woman in his life who inspires and leads him like a star. If he who seeks it, falls by the wayside during his quest, which at least is understandable, his lapses should be forgiven."

"By whom?"

"I suppose the right answer to that is God," the Marquis said a little wryly, "but I am asking for your forgiveness Tarina."

"For what you . . suggested to . . me?"

"No, for what I made you think. If I had known, as I should have done, what you were like and what you felt, I would rather have lost my right arm than spoil anything so perfect and so untouched."

Because he spoke in a way quite different from what she had ever heard before, Tarina looked at him in surprise, and he said:

"It is true, is it not, that you have never been kissed?"

"Of course I have not," Tarina said, sharply turning away from him again.

She would have taken her hand from his, but he would not let it go.

"That is what I thought," he said, "so let us start again from the very beginning. Leave everything to me. I will find a way so that we shall not lose each other, although for the moment I find it a little difficult."

"And . . Lady Bradwell?"

There was silence before the Marquis said:

"Perhaps I should make this quite clear: I have been a bachelor for a very long time, and have been quite content to remain so."

Tarina thought that Betty would be disappointed, but because of the way the Marquis spoke she felt there was nothing she could do about it.

At the same time, she was still afraid that on the homeward journey Betty might behave in the same way as Lady Millicent had.

Then she told herself that was impossible.

Betty was not like that. Though she had talked about the Count and the Prince in Rome, Tarina was sure she had not allowed them to become her lovers.

If she had flirted with them, that was understandable

because she was so lovely. But for a married woman even that would seem wrong in her father's eyes.

Quite suddenly she felt lost, like a child crying alone in a desert, without the security of a home, family, of anybody to cling to.

Because at this moment the Marquis's hand holding hers was like a lifeline in a rough sea, she held onto him.

"I . . I do not . . understand," she whispered.

There was no need for her to explain. He looked at her, then said:

"Leave everything to me. I will solve all the problems. Just trust me."

It flashed through her mind that he had been the one who was untrustworthy in the first place, but because he asked it of her, she knew she gave him her trust.

She could feel the vibrations passing from his hand to hers.

She knew as she looked at him that just as he knew what she was thinking, she could trust him.

He would in his own way find a solution to the situation which was perturbing her.

"I will sweep away everything that is ugly," he said in his deep voice.

"I want you to do . . that," she answered, "and now that Papa is . . dead, I am . . afraid."

"When we get back to the yacht," the Marquis said, "as soon as you get a chance, go and look at my pictures. You will know what they are saying to you, and it is what I shall try to say too."

Tarina gave a little sigh, but this time it was one of relief.

It suddenly struck her that if the Marquis should put his arms round her and hold her close to him, she would feel safe and protected from everything else in the world.

As she thought of it she felt the vibrations passing from his hand to hers intensify.

They seemed to move up her arm and into her breast, and she could feel them there as though they were part of the beat of her heart.

Then as she saw the jetty of the Oriental Palace ahead of

113

them she knew that what she was feeling was love!

It was hers when she least expected it, and yet so vital, so alive, it was like a streak of lightning, invading her body and imprisoning her.

. . . .

There was no sign of the Marquis at breakfast and when Betty enquired where he was, one of the stewards said that he was breakfasting in his own cabin.

She looked across the table to smile at Harry Prestwood, thinking that he would be amused, as she was, because it was so unusual.

Then she realised that Harry was not looking at her, but watching the boats on the river as if they were more interesting than she was.

Since arriving in Bangkok they had taken their meals outside in a part of the deck arranged with an awning over it, at the stern.

While Betty enjoyed watching the endless traffic up and down the waterway she felt resentful that it held Harry's interest as she was apparently unable to do.

They were alone, and suddenly she put down her knife and fork with a little bang on the table as she said to attract his attention:

"Harry!"

He did not turn his head, but merely asked:

"What is it?"

"What is wrong?"

"Who said anything was wrong?"

"I did! Ever since we have been here, in fact before we arrived, you seem to have been avoiding me. What have I done, what have I said to upset you?"

"It is nothing like that."

"I know there is something wrong."

"I do not want to talk about it."

"I do!" Betty insisted. "We were such friends, at least I thought we were, when we were travelling through the Mediterranean, the Suez Canal and the Red Sea. Now you have changed."

Harry did not speak, and after a moment she said pathetically:

"Please tell me. I have been worrying about it, and it makes me unhappy."

For the first time Harry turned his head from the river to look at her.

"Do you mean that?"

"Of course I mean it! How can you be so . . unkind?"

There was an unmistakable little break on the last word, and Harry suddenly got up from the table and said:

"I have to talk to you, but not here."

"Then where?"

"Somewhere where we will not be disturbed."

He looked to the shore on the other side of the yacht and said:

"Come with me now, quickly, before the Loraines come down for breakfast."

Betty looked at him in a bewildered fashion.

"Now? Just as I am?"

"We are only going into the garden, you will not need a hat."

The way he spoke was so urgent and at the same time so strange that Betty did not argue.

She could only follow him along the deck and over the small gangway to the jetty.

At the end of it they could walk through a gate into the garden of the Oriental Palace.

Harry opened it for her and because it was still so early there was no one about.

They moved under the trees to a secluded place among the flowering shrubs where they were sheltered by trees overhead and could not be seen by anybody passing, unless they were directly in front of them.

There was a wooden seat there on which Betty sat down and Harry did the same.

It seemed to her that he was deliberately not sitting as near to her as he might have done and she looked at him enquiringly.

However he said nothing and just stared ahead as he had done in the yacht.

"What is the matter, Harry?" she asked at last.

"You do not know?"

"I have no idea!"

He gave a deep sigh.

"I have somehow got to get home from here in another ship, or else by land."

He spoke harshly and she stared at him in astonishment.

"Why?" she asked. "What has happened?"

"I should have thought you might have guessed."

"But I have not. I do not know why you are behaving as you are. Oh, Harry, what have I done wrong?"

It was like the cry of a child that had been hurt and instantly Harry turned to her.

"For God's sake, my darling," he said, "do not speak like that. I cannot stand it!"

Betty was still in sheer surprise and he went on:

"I love you! I thought you might have guessed that. If you think I can travel back with you in 'The Sea Siren' without going mad and throwing myself overboard you are very much mistaken!"

"So that is it!" Betty exclaimed in a rapt little voice. "Why did you not tell me so? I love you too, Harry! I have loved you for weeks and have been so unhappy because I thought you were . . indifferent towards . . me."

"Indifferent?" Harry said with a groan.

As if he could not help himself he turned towards her and taking her hands in his, covered them with kisses.

"I adore you! I worship you!" he said. "It has been a hell no man should pass through to see you looking so exquisitely beautiful and to know that there was never a chance in a million years of you belonging to me."

"But . . why should you . . say that?"

"Because you were brought here to amuse Vivien, and because I have nothing to offer you."

"N.nothing?"

Harry's fingers tightened on hers until they were bloodless.

"Do you suppose if I had been able to ask you to marry me I would not have done so in the first few days after we met?"

She did not answer and after a moment he went on:

"It is not only because you are the most beautiful person I have ever seen in my life, but because everything about you is as lovely as your face – your sweetness, your understanding, your sympathy."

He sighed before he continued:

"I could go on talking about you for years, but still I have to go away from you because I cannot bear it any more."

"Why? Why?" Betty asked.

He released her hands and once again was staring with sightless eyes across the garden before he said:

"I possess nothing – nothing! My father is running up astronomical debts which I suppose somehow I shall have to meet when he dies, and if it were not for Vivien, I imagine I might easily starve or find myself in prison for debt!"

Betty gave a little cry of horror.

"But – surely there is something you can do?"

"If you tell me what it is, I will do it."

There was silence, then he went on:

"Ever since I knew I loved you I have laid awake thinking up impossible, mad schemes to enable me to ask you to be my wife."

Betty made a little sound but did not interrupt and he went on:

"But there is no way that I can get any money without sponging on my friends, which I have no intention of doing, especially Vivien, or becoming a road-sweeper. My education has made me fit for nothing else!"

He spoke so bitterly that Betty put out her hand and laid it on his arm.

"Please, Harry, do not be so . . unhappy."

"How can I be anything else when I love you?" he asked. "Oh, God, why did this have to happen to me? I have known many women, and I will not pretend to you that they have not amused and intrigued me, but I have never wanted one of them to be my wife, or to be in my life forever, until I met you."

There was silence. Then Betty said:

"I know you are very – proud, Harry – but I shall have some money – even if I marry again."

"I have thought of that," Harry said, "but do you think we could build a marriage on a complete lack of honour and self-respect? That is how I would feel if I lived on my wife's money, and had none of my own."

"It would not be a great deal, Harry. My husband left me in trust everything he possessed, but if I marry again I will have only a quarter of what I have now."

"If it were only a few shillings it would be too much, unless I could equal it with money of my own," Harry replied. "Besides how do you think I would feel if you could not have all the comforts you have now, and the gowns that make you look even more beautiful than you are already?"

"Do you think any of that matters," Betty asked, "as long as I could have you? My darling, I would be quite happy to be with you in a tent, or to sleep in a barn. I have – never felt like this about – anybody in my life – before."

The way she spoke made Harry look at her.

Then with a sigh that was half one of exaltation and half one of utter despair, he pulled her into his arms and his lips sought hers.

He kissed her passionately, insistently, demandingly. Then he said in a voice that was curiously unsteady:

"My precious, how I love you for what you have just said, but the answer is 'no!' Positively and absolutely 'No!' "

"Why?" Betty cried. "Why?"

"You have already taken the social world by storm," Harry replied. "Enjoy yourself and just forget there is a fool called 'Harry Prestwood', who will love you until he dies."

"Please, Harry, I cannot bear it!" Betty said. "I want you to stay with me – I want to be with you – how can I – lose you?"

"You are very young," Harry answered. "There will be dozens of men in your life, and among them you will find somebody you will love and who obviously will love you, but I cannot bear to think about it."

"I thought when I was widowed," Betty said, "that I would never marry again because I had been so . . unhappy. But now I want to – marry you, Harry. I want to be your – wife, and honestly money does not – matter to me."

118

"It matters to me!" Harry said. "When you are so beautiful, how could I drag you into the shabbiness and humiliation of being so poor that we would always have to sponge off our friends or else literally go hungry?"

He drew a deep breath.

"My darling, my lovely one, take care of yourself. When we go back to the yacht I am going to borrow enough money from Vivien, which I doubt if I shall ever be able to repay, to go back to England on the next ship which calls here. The fare will very likely be cheaper that way than if I go by land."

"Oh, Harry, do not talk like that," Betty pleaded. "Please – stay with me – at least for a little while – so that we can talk about – ourselves."

"It is no use, darling," Harry said. "Because I love you, it is going to be agony even to look at you and know that I cannot make you mine."

"Supposing – just supposing – that when you – go away – I insist upon coming with you?" Betty asked in a small voice. "You – need not marry me – but at least – we can be together."

There was silence. Then Harry said angrily:

"You are not to speak like that! Do you suppose I have not thought of that and then have been ashamed at my own thoughts?"

He took her hand in his again.

"You are not one of the 'Lady Millicents' of this world, Betty. You are much too good, pure and decent in every way."

His eyes studied her face as he said:

"You were meant to be a man's wife, and the mother of his children, and I hate to think of you being part of the spoiled, sophisticated, immoral Society into which Vivien will undoubtedly take you."

"He will take me – nowhere!" Betty cried, "when I might be with – you."

"I adore you, my precious one, for what you have suggested," Harry said, "but the answer is 'No!' You have no idea how different you are from all the other women with whom Vivien and I have enjoyed ourselves, and I will not have you spoiled."

He put down her hands as he finished speaking and kissed her fingers one by one, then turned one hand over and kissed the palm passionately and insistently.

"Supposing," Betty said in a very small voice, "when you are – not there I do become – spoiled – hard and – immoral like Lady Millicent?"

Harry looked into her eyes.

"I want you to promise me, my precious one, that it will be something you will never do," he said. "Promise me on everything you hold sacred, and on our love that you will remain as you are now, until you find some decent man who will enshrine you in his heart as you are enshrined in mine."

"I promise," Betty whispered, "because I shall never – find such a – man. The only person in my heart – Harry, is you, and I know, just as if – God was telling me so – that I shall never love – anybody else."

She saw the pain in his eyes before he put his arms around her and kissed her.

He kissed her in a different way from before, slowly, possessively and at the same time as if she was something very sacred and he revered her.

Then he said with a brief smile:

"This is goodbye, my darling. I shall not touch you again before I leave, and I will not even dare to talk to you alone. Remember what I have said to you. Whatever happens in the future, just remember that if you do anything wrong you will be spoiling the image of you that I hold in my heart and in my soul."

"Oh – Harry! How can – you say such – things?" Betty asked.

Now the tears were running down her face and she made no effort to wipe them away.

"I love you! I love – you!"

"And I will love you through all eternity."

He looked at her for a long moment as if he would imprint her loveliness on his mind.

Then he turned and walked away, leaving her alone in the garden.

CHAPTER SEVEN

When Tarina got back to the yacht she went to her cabin feeling as though the world had turned upside-down, and she had no idea what she could do about it.

She only knew that her whole being went out to the Marquis because she loved him.

At the same time her mind told her that what he was envisaging and suggesting was wrong and wicked, and she must have nothing to do with him.

Then her whole body became a battle-ground and there was a war in her breast which seemed to tear her apart.

"I love him!" she whispered in the silence of her small cabin. "But he will never . . understand that I cannot . . behave like Lady Millicent. It would horrify Papa and Mama!"

She was not certain exactly what it was that the Marquis was suggesting to her, except that in some way he wanted her to behave towards him as Lady Millicent had.

He had been right when he said that her love which was like the stars which on the ground would only be reflected and distorted.

Because she loved him she tried to make excuses for what he was suggesting, but she knew even as she did so that it was impossible to explain away what was a sin.

She sat down on her bed and thought that if her father was alive she could go to him with her troubles and he would not only explain it all to her, but tell her what to do.

But she was alone, completely and absolutely alone, there was no one to whom she could turn for help, and the only thing left was her prayers.

Even as she prayed with an up-lifting of her whole self for help and guidance, she knew that her heart pulled her in a very different direction because of her love.

"How can I . . love him? How can it have . . happened so suddenly?" Tarina asked herself.

She knew if she was honest that the Marquis had had a strange effect on her from the first moment she had seen him, when his voice seemed to vibrate within her.

Her mind and spirit had responded to him so that now she felt that even if they never saw each other again, they were joined in some mystic manner which the Buddhists would say could only be explained by the 'Wheel of Re-birth'.

She felt her mind going to his pictures and responding to the beauty of them as he told her to do.

"Because he understands them, surely he . . realises that there is no . . question of my playing . . any part in . . his life?" Tarina argued to herself.

She had only to think of the Marquis sitting beside her as they were rowed down the river to feel a throbbing within her breast and the inescapable conviction that even though he was not touching her they were joined to one another.

"What can I . . do?" she asked desperately. "Oh, Mama what . . can I . . do?"

There seemed to be no answer and when she looked at the clock she realised that in a few minutes time she must call Betty.

She took off her hat, smoothed her hair without bothering to look in the mirror, then moved quietly along the corridor to Betty's cabin.

The curtains were drawn, and as the sunshine swept in through the portholes she saw that Betty was lying against her pillows, but her eyes were open.

She did not speak and Tarina tidied some clothes away before she asked:

"Is there anything you would like?"

"No, I want nothing," Betty replied.

She sounded rather depressed and Tarina wondered what was wrong but thought it might annoy her if she asked questions.

122

Instead she told the steward that Betty was awake and he carried a large can of hot water for her to the cabin-door.

He was cheery and rather cheeky as Hunt usually was in the morning, but Tarina found it almost impossible to answer him.

Then as she went back into Betty's cabin she had a sudden idea.

'I must go away,' she thought. 'It is no use staying here fighting against the Marquis when I am sure that I shall be . . defeated.'

Betty seemed to have little to say and they hardly talked while she was dressing, and once she had gone on deck to have breakfast, Tarina went back to her own cabin.

It was then the idea of going away returned to her and she was quite certain that was what she must do.

"How can I stay with the Marquis . . see him and hear his voice . . without sooner or later agreeing to what he suggests?" she asked.

She was not absolutely certain what he wanted except that vaguely at the back of her mind she had heard that rich aristocrats like the Marquis offered their 'protection' to actresses and dancers, who became their mistresses.

She also knew that the Kings of France had very beautiful mistresses who held acknowledged positions at Court.

When she had read about *Madame* de Pompadour and *Madame* de Maintenon, who had played a part in the history of France, they had just been stories with which she had never for one moment connected herself.

It was like reading about the Crusades, and not having any idea of the suffering and the agonies of death which happened to ordinary men.

When she had read with her father about the customs and religions of other countries and the beauty of the Himalayas, they had seemed very real and something she could understand in detail.

But because she had been brought up so quietly and with no contact with men outside the Parish except a few elderly gentlemen, everything that appertained to love was unreal and did not touch her personally.

She actually had no idea what a man and a woman did when they 'made love'.

She thought now that one of the reasons she had been so shocked when she had realised that the Marquis was the lover of Lady Millicent was that it was he who was playing such a part.

Even when she had only spoken to him once, seen him in the distance and heard his voice, he had already meant something to her.

Now she supposed when she learned that he was making love to a married woman it had affected her more than if it had been another man in whom she had no interest.

Because she had a sharp and logical brain, Tarina faced the truth and did not prevaricate.

For her to love the Marquis was to look up at a star, as he had told her to do, but to know that it was completely and absolutely out of reach.

Therefore to yearn after him, to long for the closeness of him and be affected by his vibrations was only to make herself miserable.

What was more, she might eventually succumb, because she could not help it, to the intimacy he desired and which she knew was wicked unless they were married.

'I must go away!' she thought.

It might be a solution of weakness, but she was afraid that her love would prevent her from seeing clearly what was right and what was wrong.

"I must be brave," she told herself, "although it will be agonising to leave him."

Her courage came from a very long line of ancestors who had fought not only for their country, but also as her father had done, for what was right and good, against what was wrong and evil.

She found a new determination within herself that she had not had before and soon after Betty had gone out on deck for breakfast, she decided:

"I will ask her to lend me enough money to go home."

She was well aware there were quite a number of ships passing up and down the river, and she was sure one of them would take her back to England without it costing her very much.

Then she knew she would have to give an explanation as to why she wanted to leave, but it would be a mistake to tell Betty the truth.

This created a new difficulty, and she sat thinking of what excuse she could make to go home without revealing that she was running away from the Marquis.

'Betty loves him,' Tarina thought, 'and perhaps despite what he said about wishing to remain a bachelor, he will fall in love with her.'

It seemed to her incredible that anybody would not love Betty when she was so beautiful and such a very sweet person.

Then almost as if the Marquis was beside her arguing with her she knew the answer was that Betty did not feel as she did about the *Jatakas*.

It was that and the vibrations between them that had set him and herself apart from other people.

"At the same time," she said defiantly, "he is the Marquis of Oakenshaw and, as far as he is concerned, I am a servant."

Once again she knew he was a star out of reach, and even to go on looking at him was a mistake.

"What can I do? Oh, Papa, tell me what I can do!" she asked aloud.

But while there was no answer from her father she could almost hear the Marquis's deep voice saying:

"Trust me."

It was very quiet and Tarina was sitting and thinking in her cabin when quite suddenly she heard the patter of footsteps coming down the companionway and running past her door, and she knew it was Betty going to her cabin.

She heard the slam of the door, and because she had been in such a hurry Tarina felt there must be something wrong.

Quickly she walked to Betty's cabin and went in without knocking.

Betty was lying face downwards on the bed crying tempestuously, as if her heart would break.

125

"Dearest, what is the matter?" Tarina asked in consternation. "Tell me, please tell me what has upset you."

Betty did not answer. She just went on sobbing and Tarina sat down on the edge of the mattress and put her arms around her.

"You must not cry like this," she said. "You will make yourself ill. What has happened?"

For some minutes it was impossible for Betty to speak. Then in a voice that was almost incoherent she said:

"H.Harry – is – leaving!"

"Harry?"

"I – I shall – never see him – again!" Betty sobbed. "I love him – oh, Tarina – I love – him – so much!"

"You said – Harry?" Tarina asked, but Betty went on as if she had not spoken:

"I – wanted to – go with him but he will not – let me – and I do not – think I can live – without him."

Once again there was a burst of sobs and Tarina, bewildered but concerned, could only hold her closer and say:

"Please, dearest, do not cry. Tell me what happened, and perhaps I can help."

"N.no one can – help," Betty answered. "He – loves me – and I – love him! Oh, Tarina, – I wish I were – dead!"

She cried so tempestuously that her whole body shook with emotion and grief.

Tarina could only hold her close and talk to her soothingly, feeling as she did so that this was something she had never anticipated.

She had been so certain that Betty was concentrating, as she had said she intended to do, on the Marquis, that it had never occurred to her that it might be Harry Prestwood with whom she fell in love.

Tarina had seen him moving about on deck and thought he was very handsome, and at the beginning of their voyage Betty had talked about him quite a lot, telling her the amusing things he had said and the compliments he had paid her.

Tarina had been glad that Harry was there to take Betty's mind off the Marquis and Lady Millicent.

She thought in fact that it was very tactful of Harry to divert Betty from being upset by the Marquis's behaviour.

Now she realised that after they left Calcutta Betty had seemed quieter and at times depressed, and this mood had seemed to be accentuated day by day.

"Tarina – what am I to – do?" Betty asked now.

Very gently Tarina laid her back against the pillows and said:

"I am going to get some cold water to wash your eyes, and you must not cry any more."

"It – does not matter – what I look – like, if – Harry is not there," Betty replied. "Oh, – Tarina – I love him so desperately – I would follow him bare-foot from here to – England – if he would allow me to . . ."

"Have you told him that?"

"Of course I told him! But although he said – he would love me all his life – he also said that we must – never see each other again – and I cannot – bear it!"

Her voice broke on the last words and her tears fell unchecked down her cheeks.

Not knowing how to comfort her, Tarina fetched a bowl of cold water and a small sponge and brought them to the side of the bed.

Because Betty seemed incapable of doing anything, she washed her eyes and dried them with a soft towel, but almost as soon as she had done so, the tears were back again.

"I told him I would – live with him in a – tent," Betty said, "or a barn – as long as we could be together – but he would not – have me – Oh – Harry – Harry! How can I go on living without – you?"

. . . .

Harry had returned from the garden and gone straight to the Marquis's cabin.

He found him sitting at his desk writing and he looked up as Harry entered to say rather abruptly:

"I am busy, Harry!"

"I want to tell you something and it is very important," Harry answered.

The Marquis put down his pen and looked up at his friend without the usual smile of welcome on his face.

"What is wrong?" he asked.

There was a little pause before Harry replied:

"I have come, Vivien, to ask you to lend me enough money to return home on a ship or over land, whichever is the cheapest, and it is likely to be a long time before I can repay you."

He spoke in a hard, controlled voice as if he was forcing the words from his lips.

The Marquis looked at him in sheer astonishment.

"Do I understand that you wish to leave?" he asked. "But why? What has happened?"

"I do not want to give any explanation," Harry replied. "I am just asking you, as I have never asked you before, to lend me some money."

The Marquis sat back in his chair.

"You can hardly expect me to be satisfied with that answer. After all, we have been friends for a long time, Harry, and if you are in any trouble you know I will stand by you."

"If I were in the sort of trouble you are thinking of, I would tell you what it was, knowing that you would not fail me. But at the moment there is nothing you can do except give me what I ask."

"Do not be such a fool, Harry!" the Marquis exclaimed. "You know I will lend you any money you want. At the same time, as you are a friend, I want to know the reason for your sudden aversion to my company."

"It is not that, you know it is not that," Harry said, "but Vivien, I have to go away. There is nothing else I can do."

The Marquis was silent for a moment. Then he asked:

"Does your reason for such a hasty departure concern Betty Bradwell?"

"I told you, I do not want to talk about it."

"Knowing you as well as I do," the Marquis said, "I thought you seemed very enamoured of her until we reached Calcutta. Then you appeared to cool off."

"You asked me to keep her amused because you were

128

otherwise engaged,'' Harry replied, ''and seeing how much I owe you, I tried to behave honourably.''

''But you have fallen in love?''

Harry did not have to answer the Marquis's question the expression on his face doing it for him.

The Marquis smiled.

''Good! I am delighted! And, Harry, if you are trying to be loyal to me and all that sort of thing, forget it! I think Betty is very beautiful, but I am not interested in her.''

To his surprise the expression of grim despair on Harry's face did not disappear, and he merely said abruptly:

''I have to leave, Vivien.''

''Why? Has she turned you down? In which case you have the whole return voyage in which to try again.

Harry walked across the cabin to stand at the porthole.

''I suppose you had better know the truth, Vivien,'' he said. ''She is the only woman I have ever met whom I wish to be my wife, but you know my circumstances better than anyone else. So the only decent thing I can do is to get out of her life as fast as possible.''

''You are quite certain that you love her like that?'' the Marquis asked very quietly.

''As certain as I am that I am alive and that without her the future is darker than Hell!''

''Then surely . . .?'' the Marquis began.

Harry turned from the port-hole to interrupt him saying:

''You do not suppose I have not thought out all the possibilities? Yes, I know she has some money, but I will not touch it. Yes, I know I might be an Agent on one of your estates, but do you think that is the sort of life I could offer to someone as beautiful as Betty?''

He waited for the Marquis to reply and when he did not do so, he went on:

''How could I drag her down to the level of your friends who always have their hands in your pockets for something, make her struggle to keep a house going without sufficient servants, and bring up our children without being able to pay for their education?''

''You might both be very happy,'' the Marquis remarked.

"And how would I feel if I saw her slaving away and having none of the things she has now? And perhaps growing to hate me when she remembers the social success she was before I married her."

"Have you said all this to Betty?"

"She said she would live with me in a tent or a barn as long as we could be together," Harry said. "That is the sort of woman she is, I want to kneel at her feet because she is so different."

"So it is your pride that makes you throw away something which I should have thought was unique," the Marquis said dryly.

"How can I do anything else?"

"There must be other alternatives."

"And what are they? You better than anybody else know that when my father dies a mountain of debts will hang around my neck like a millstone until I die too!"

"Take a chance," the Marquis said quietly. "I am sure that somehow with your courage and intelligence, Harry, you can make a go of it."

"You must be mad!"

Then he stared at the Marquis and said:

"You are not saying what I expected you to say in the circumstances!"

"What would that be?"

"That I should take what the gods have offered and make Betty mine without worrying about the future."

"Then why do you not do that?"

"Because," Harry said raising his voice and speaking very seriously, "I love her too much to drag her down to the level of Millicent Carson and dozens like her with whom we have amused ourselves in the past."

He paused and drew in his breath before he went on:

"At the moment she is young, unspoilt, and completely unawakened to what love can mean between a man and a woman. I love her too much to make her like one of those other women who have amused us for a short while before we forget them."

Harry spoke violently, then as if embarrassed by his lack

130

of control he turned again to the port-hole to say in a different tone of voice:

"For God's sake, Vivien, lend me the money and let me go!"

"Of course I will give you anything you want," the Marquis answered, "but I think you are making a mistake. If Betty loves you as much as you love her, then you are both crucifying yourselves unnecessarily."

"That is our business."

As he spoke the Marquis had the feeling that Harry had reached the end of his tether and it was impossible for him to stand much more.

He therefore opened a drawer in his desk and drew out a cheque-book.

"I can lend you £1,000," he said, "but do not struggle to give it back too quickly!"

Harry did not answer and the Marquis went on:

"I only hope that as you travel home in some uncomfortable stinking steamship you will come to your senses, and I shall find you waiting for us at one of the ports of call on our homeward journey."

"You will not find me there, but at home," Harry said quickly. "I am going to see if I can salvage anything from the wreck my father has made of it."

The way he spoke told the Marquis it was useless to argue any further.

He wrote out a cheque for £1,000, signed his name, and put it on the desk in front of him.

As he did so, Harry turned slowly from the port-hole almost as if he was reluctant to take it.

Then even as he put out his hand to pick it up the door of the cabin opened and one of the stewards came in.

"What is it, Jenkins?" the Marquis asked sharply.

"It's a cablegram, M'Lord, brought from the British Consulate for Mr. Prestwood. I thought 'e should 'ave it immediately!"

As he spoke the steward walked across the cabin with the cablegram and handed it to Harry. Then as the steward left the cabin he looked at it in surprise.

131

"I can think of only one reason why I should receive a cablegram here in Bangkok," he said in a low voice.

"That your father is dead? I will take you home as quickly as possible," the Marquis said.

Slowly, as if he was reluctant to know the worst, Harry opened the cablegram.

The Marquis watched his face as he read it, and knew without being told what it contained.

Harry read it through, then read it again as if to confirm that he was not mistaken, before he gave sudden shout that seemed to echo round the walls.

He threw the cablegram at the Marquis, and pulling open the door ran down the corridor.

For a moment the Marquis was so astonished by his behaviour that he could only stare after him.

Then he picked up the cablegram from where Harry had thrown it on the desk and read:

"Edward Prestwood Esq.,
c/o The Marquis of Oakenshaw,
S.Y. The Sea Siren,
The British Legation,
Bangkok,
Siam.

We deeply regret to inform you that your father Sir Roger Prestwood, Baronet, died yesterday afternoon from a heart-attack brought on by the news that he had won a Lottery in South America whose value in sterling is approximately £200,000. The Funeral will be on Saturday and we beg that you will return as speedily as possible to deal with many urgent matters concerning the estate.
Respectfully yours,
Mayhew, Martin and Mayhew."

Just as Harry had done, the Marquis read through the cablegram a second time to see that there was no mistake. Then he rose to his feet to follow his friend.

· · · · · · ·

There were still tears in Betty's eyes, but she was no longer crying so convulsively.

As Tarina put the bowl of water back on the washstand she asked:

"What am I - to do - Tarina? I can no - longer think and - I am so - unhappy . . ."

She did not finish the sentence for the door of the cabin burst open and Harry stood there.

For a moment he just looked at her and Betty sat up and put out her hands towards him.

"Harry!"

He did not speak, he only went on looking at her.

Then as if he forced himself to walk slowly he moved towards the bed and sat down facing her.

Her hands were out-stretched, her eyes raised to his as she pleaded with him wordlessly. Then he said hoarsely:

"Everything is all right, my darling! How soon will you marry me?"

"Harry!"

It was like the cry of a lark flying up into the sky.

"My father is dead and instead of debts he has left me a fortune!"

It was impossible for Betty to speak, for she was crying again, but now there were tears of happiness.

Harry pulled her close against him, and held her as if he would never let her go.

Standing on the other side of the cabin Tarina could only stare at them, feeling that since Betty had been saved at the last moment her Guardian Angel must have been watching over her.

"I love you!" Harry said. "Now we can be married here before we return home, and there will be no more problems, no more unhappiness."

"I cannot - believe - it!" Betty said in a broken voice.

"It is true! It is true! We can be together, my precious one, with no more partings and no more tears!"

He turned her face up to his as he spoke and his lips were on hers.

Watching them kiss Tarina came out of her trance and thinking for the first time that she should leave them alone, she started towards the door.

Only as she reached it did Betty see her and holding out her hand said:

"Oh, Tarina – do not go! There can be no – secrets from Harry and we – must tell him why you are – here – and how much you – mean to me."

Tarina ran towards the bed.

"The only thing that matters," she said, "is that now you can be happy, Dearest, and that is wonderful!"

She kissed Betty on the cheek, and Harry asked:

"What is this secret you have been keeping from me?"

"Tarina is my first cousin," Betty replied, "and I love her very much, and I want you to love her too."

"And so I shall," Harry answered, "but at the moment, my darling, I can think of no one but you."

They looked at each other and were lost in a world of their own.

Tactfully Tarina moved away to leave the cabin and only as she looked towards the door did she realise that what Betty had said had been overheard.

The Marquis was standing there looking at the dramatic scene taking place with what she thought was an undoubted twinkle in his eyes.

Because even to see him made her heart turn over in her breast and she found it difficult to breathe, she could only stand staring at him.

It was impossible to leave the cabin as he was in the doorway, and Betty and Harry were quite oblivious for the moment of anything except themselves.

"I feel, Tarina, that we are decidedly *de trop*," the Marquis said quietly.

He stepped aside for her to pass him and shut the door behind them.

As she waited in the passage a little uncertain and wondering whether she should go to her own cabin, he said.

"Come with me. I want to talk to you."

Then, as if once again the world had turned upside-down Tarina went to his study, where the pictures, now standing on the floor propped against the bookcases, seemed to glow at her like a light.

As she turned to look at the Marquis he said:

"So at last this formidable secret has been revealed, and you are Betty Bradwell's cousin!"

"Y.yes."

"Why did you have to pretend to be her lady's-maid?"

Tarina looked at him apprehensively, in case he was angry.

"My father died . . I have no money and I went to London to find . . employment."

The Marquis raised his eye-brows, but he did not speak and she went on:

"I needed a reference, and although I had not seen Betty for two years because she had been living abroad, I knew she would give me one."

"But instead she engaged you."

"Her lady's-maid had broken her leg, and it seemed a . . Heaven-sent opportunity for me to . . come to Siam."

The Marquis laughed.

"Just as simple as that. I have lain awake at night imagining all sorts of reasons why you should be in disguise, and why you should be dressed as no lady's-maid could possibly afford to be."

"Betty gave me all the clothes she had been wearing when she was in mourning."

"A very simple explanation," the Marquis said, "and very far from the one which tortured me and made me very jealous."

Because of the way he spoke, Tarina felt herself blush.

"Now we have 'cleared the decks'," he said, "and as Betty and Harry are intent on getting married in Bangkok before they leave for home, I suggest we had better do the same."

For a moment Tarina felt she could not have heard him aright, then because she was sure she must have been mistaken she said almost beneath her breath;

"Are you . . asking me to . . marry you?"

"I am saying that I intend to marry you!" the Marquis answered. "I told you to trust me."

"But you said you . . wanted to . . remain a bachelor . . and had . . no intention of . . marrying."

"That was true until I met you."

There was silence. The Marquis did not move and Tarina did not look at him. Then she said in a very small voice:

"Are you . . asking me to . . marry you . . only because you now . . know I am . . Betty's cousin?"

The Marquis smiled.

"I might have guessed your sharp little brain would not have missed that as an explanation. So in order to convince you I will show you the letter I have just finished writing to the Foreign Secretary, Lord Rosebery."

It was lying on the open blotter on his desk. He had finished it when Harry interrupted him, except for the signature.

He picked it up and handed it to Tarina, but she hesitated as she took it from him and he said:

"Read it, I want you to."

Obediently she looked down at the piece of paper in her hand, and read:

> *"Dear Archibald,*
>
> *I enclose a report for your files on what I have said to the King, and I am quite certain that your anxieties where he is concerned have now been cleared up.*
>
> *I have also persuaded him to visit England and perhaps other countries in Europe either next year or the year after. It is something he is anxious to do, and I have promised him a very warm welcome to England.*
>
> *With regard to myself and the flattering suggestions you made to me before I left, forget them. This has indeed been a 'Voyage of Discovery', and as the 'star' I searched for is now within reach, I am to be married.*
>
> *For reasons I will explain another time this will preclude my taking up any position except that of a very happy man, and a very contented husband.*
>
> *With my good wishes, and I shall hope to receive yours in due course.*
>
> > *Yours. . . . . . . "*

Tarina read the letter through, then to her surprise the Marquis took it from her and tore it in half, throwing the pieces down on the floor.

"I shall have to write another letter to the Foreign Secretary," he said, "saying that I shall look forward to hearing what post he has in mind for me, and my wife will help me to fulfil my duties, besides, I hope, making me happy."

As he spoke he put his arms around Tarina and drew her close to him.

"I cannot believe," he said, "you will have any objections."

Tarina raised her eyes to his.

"But you . . must not marry . . me!"

"Why not? I thought you loved me."

"I love you. I love you with every breath I breathe . . but you did not . . wish to marry."

"I have fought against marriage for many years," the Marquis said, "but when we came back this morning from the Floating Market I knew that as I could not live without you there was no other way we could be together."

He bent his head so that his lips were very near to hers, but Tarina put up both her hands to press against his chest, and said:

"Please . . wait! I . . love you . . and . . also in a strange way I feel as if I already belong to you . . but I am not sure I do not . . think you . . ought to . . marry me."

"What other way do you suggest we can be together?" the Marquis asked.

"I am not . . certain . . because you are so important . . that I am . . essential to you."

The Marquis laughed, and it was a very joyous sound.

"Now you are being ridiculous," he said. "You know as well as I do that we think the same, we feel the same, we are the same! We are one person already, Tarina, and it is doubtful if marriage can make us any closer spiritually."

He drew in his breath. Then he said:

"At the same time, my darling, I want you not only as a 'Deva' but as a woman, and I can no longer go on pretending that you are not the other half of me, part of my life, now and for ever."

Tarina gave a little gasp.

Then before she could speak the Marquis pulled her closer against him and his lips were on hers.

As he kissed her she knew it was what she had been longing and yearning for, and his kiss was more wonderful than she had ever imagined in her dreams.

As his lips held her captive she felt as if the warmth of the sun was moving through her whole body, burning through her breasts and up her neck, onto her lips, which then gave their warmth to his.

As he held her closer still she knew that the vibrations she had felt ever since she first met him seemed to join with hers until they were, as he had already said, one person.

Yet his kisses were more than that.

She had never thought it possible to feel such ecstasy such rapture, as if he swept her into the sky and there were no problems, no troubles, but only a divine happiness that was beyond words and almost beyond thought.

When the Marquis raised his head she said a little incoherently:

"I love you . . I . . love you! I did not . . know that love could be so . . wonderful!"

"Nor did I," he replied. "Oh, my darling, suppose I had lost you?"

Then he was kissing her again, kissing her passionately, demandingly until the sensations he aroused in her were so intense that she felt that she must have reached Heaven and could never return to earth again.

. . . .

A long time later the Marquis said:

"How can I have been so fortunate as to find what I have been seeking all my life waiting for me in my own yacht?"

"You could hardly have . . expected to find your wife in the . . guise of a . . lady's-maid."

"I never for one moment believed you were really that," the Marquis replied. "When I first saw you looking at me from the darkness of the deck with the moonlight on your face I thought you were a vision or a spectre come to haunt me."

He kissed her forehead and went on:

"Then I knew I had never seen anybody so beautiful or so

exquisite, and you must have dropped from the sky.''

Tarina did not answer. She hid her face against his neck and he said:

"I know now you are on earth. At the same time, my darling, though I passed through all the temptations thought up by the evil demons, I shall be an exemplary husband."

He smiled very tenderly before he ordered:

"I can promise you one thing: because you are so beautiful, because there is something between us which has never happened with anybody else, from now on there will be no temptations in my life."

"I . . hope that is . . true," Tarina said, "I love you with all my heart . . and I want to . . inspire you . . and make you . . sure that I am the . . star you have been seeking . . and not just a . . reflection of it in a . . muddy puddle."

The Marquis laughed at his own words being quoted back at him. Then he said:

"You are everything a woman should be, and so incredibly lovely that it will take me a lifetime to tell you how beautiful you are."

Tarina looked down at the pictures on the floor. Then she said:

"I . . I am still a . . little afraid."

"Of what?"

"That I am not . . important enough to be your wife . . I am so very ignorant of the life you lead that I . . might not make you . . happy."

The Marquis held her so close to him that it was difficult to breathe. Then he said:

"I adore your ignorance, your innocence and your purity, my lovely one, and I have a great deal to teach you, just as you have a lot to teach me. I do not believe that in such circumstances we can be anything but divinely happy."

He drew her nearer to the pictures and as they looked down at them he said:

"You said they were there to teach not our minds, but our spirits, and my spirit has developed, intensified and become

139

stronger. What is more, I have a new awareness of life since I have known you.''

"Is that . . really true?" Tarina asked.

"I think your instinct would tell you if I was lying."

She gave a little sigh.

"I do not believe anyone could be so wonderful! And what you think is what Papa would want us both to think and what he would think himself."

The Marquis tightened his arms as he said:

"I thought when I first saw your cousin that she was the most beautiful woman I had ever seen, but when I saw you I knew that I was mistaken. You are infinitely more beautiful, because your beauty is not only in your face, but comes from your soul."

Tarina gave a cry.

"How can you say such marvellous things to me . . and which I long to hear?"

"As it happens I am very surprised at myself!" the Marquis smiled. "But then I have never felt in my whole life what I feel for you now."

"I am so . . lucky . . so very . . very lucky," Tarina said, "and I shall . . always be grateful to the Karma which brought us together.

She paused before she said very solemnly:

"It was my Karma which took me to Betty at exactly the right moment, when she was very excited at receiving your invitation to travel on *"The Sea Siren"*."

The Marquis did not speak, he merely moved his mouth over the softness of her skin.

Then as if he did not wish Tarina to think too much about why he had chosen his party to go with him to Siam he kissed her.

At the touch of his lips they were once again swept away by the rapture and ecstasy of love and it carried them up to the stars.

. . . .

When the Marquis and Tarina went to find Betty and Harry to tell them that they were to be married, for a

140

moment they were both stunned into silence.

Then Harry gave a shout of joy.

"I can hardly believe it!" he exclaimed. "It is the best news I have ever had!"

He turned to Tarina.

"Thank you for capturing the most elusive and most wily bachelor that ever managed to evade all the hooks and lines cast over his nose!"

The Marquis laughed.

"You are making Tarina shy," he said, "and she did not try to catch me, I caught her!"

Betty put her arms around Tarina and kissed her.

"Oh, darling, I am so glad," she said. "Harry and I are so happy that we want everybody else to be happy too."

"That is exactly the way we should feel in Siam," the Marquis said.

" 'The Land of Smiles'!" Tarina completed.

"The first thing we have to do," Harry said in a practical tone, "is to go to the British Ministry and find out where we can be married and how soon."

"I do not think there will be any difficulties about that," the Marquis replied, "and because Harry, I know you want to get home quickly, the sooner our weddings can take place the better!"

"I can imagine nothing nicer than for Tarina and me to be married in Siam," Betty said. "The only thing is, I hope we have pretty enough gowns to please two very fastidious men."

"Whatever you wear or do not wear, will please me," Harry said in a low voice.

Betty blushed and as they looked into each others eyes it was obviously impossible for them to think of anything else but each other.

As if he found it tiresome not to be able to talk to Tarina alone, the Marquis took her back to his Study.

As he did so he stopped a steward in the passage to say:

"Order a carriage to take us to the British Ministry in half-an-hour's time!"

"Very good, M'Lord!"

The steward hurried away and the Marquis drew Tarina into the cabin and shut the door behind them.

"I have half-an-hour in which to tell you how much I love you," he said.

She looked at the torn-up pieces of writing-paper lying on the floor and said:

"Perhaps I should leave you while you write another letter to Lord Rosebery."

"That can wait."

He put his arms round her and held her very close before he said:

"Now tell me you are sorry that you made me so desperately worried."

She looked at him enquiringly and he said:

"You are sensible enough to know that because I have a position of some importance in England, not just in the Social World, but as head of my family, and as the President, Patron or Founder of dozens of different organisations, I was concerned that they might not approve of my marriage."

"You are . . quite certain they will . . approve now?"

"As you know," the Marquis said, "I was prepared to give up anything so that I could marry you, my darling, but it does make things a little easier, knowing that Betty's father was a very respected Country Squire and her mother and yours belong to a family that is almost as old as mine."

"H.how do you . . know all these things?"

"I suppose I am very meticulous in my life and the way I live," the Marquis replied, "so I like to know everything about my friends before they become too important to me."

She moved away for him to say:

"And if I had . . really been the . . unknown 'Mademoiselle Janzé' from France?"

"I still intended to marry you," the Marquis answered, "because I knew that because I love you I could not lose or spoil anything so perfect and so spiritually close to me."

He gave a sigh of relief as he finished:

"At the same time, my love, the gods have been kind, for it is far easier to swim with the tide than against it."

"You . . really were . . prepared to marry . . 'Miss Nobody'?" Tarina insisted.

"I have already said that as no one has ever made me feel as you do, and no one before has ever made me aware that love is a gift from God, I could not lose anything so precious."

As the Marquis spoke, the last worry went from Tarina's eyes, and she moved towards him as if he drew her irresistibly and her arms went round his neck.

"I love you . . I love you!" she said, "but I have . . nothing to give . . you except my . . love. Will that be . . enough?"

He knew the question was very important and replied:

"It is all I want now and for ever. I think, my darling, we both know that because we in ourselves are complete we have a great deal to give to the world and to the other people who are not as fortunate as ourselves."

It was the answer she wanted. Her eyes shone with a dazzling light and as she could find no words in which to express her happiness, Tarina merely raised her lips to his.

When she could speak she said in a rapt little voice:

"Teach me . . please teach me to do everything that you want and which it is . . right for me to do."

He did not answer and she whispered:

"I may make mistakes and you will be . . ashamed of . . me."

The Marquis turned her face up to his.

"I will teach you about love my precious one," he said, "and I will also look after you and protect you so that you will never make mistakes."

His voice deepened.

"What is more important than Social protocol is that you give everyone you meet the love which I feel vibrating from you."

Then he kissed her until they were both breathless before he said:

"The carriage will be here in a few minutes, my precious love. Go and put on your hat, and as Bangkok is famous for its jewels, I intend to stop on the way to the Ministry and buy you a ring which will be another thing that will chain you to me from now until eternity.''

''That sounds very . . exciting!'' Tarina replied, ''but I would rather have your . . kisses than all the jewels in Siam . . or anywhere else for that . . matter.''

The Marquis put out his arms towards her but she evaded him and with a smile that seemed part of the sunshine she slipped out of the cabin.

He stood for a moment looking at the closed door. Then he turned and his eyes were on the *Jatakas* pictures.

''I think you have laid a spell on me,'' he said almost defiantly.

Then as if they answered with one voice they replied in his heart:

''We have led you to a star!''